The Story of the American Indian

The Story of the American Indian

Written and illustrated by
Sydney E. Fletcher

AXIOS
for Young People

Axios Press
P.O. Box 118
Mount Jackson, VA 22842
888.542.9467 info@axiospress.com

Library of Congress Cataloging-in-Publication Data

Fletcher, Sydney E.
[American Indian]
The story of the American Indian / written and illustrated by Sydney E. Fletcher.
p. cm.
Originally published: The American Indian. New York : Grosset & Dunlap, c1954.
Includes index.
ISBN 978-1-60419-032-8 (hardcover)
1. Indians of North America. I. Title.

E77.F59 2010

970.004'97—dc22

2010022401

Contents

Acknowledgments from the First Edition

Since Sydney Fletcher died before he could finish this book, the publishers wish to acknowledge the contribution of Aubrey Wells, who completed the work of illustration with all the spirit and fidelity that Mr. Fletcher could have wished.

A list of every book consulted, every museum tramped through, every picture studied, and every Indian reservation visited in the course of preparing this book would be far too long to include here. We wish especially, however, to acknowledge the help of the US Bureau of Indian Affairs, which has supplied information and photographs; of the Office of Work with Young People of the New York Public Library for their valuable suggestions; of Ms. LaVerne Madigan of the Association on American Indian Affairs, New York; and of Dr. Gordon F. Ekholm, Department of Anthropology, Museum of Natural History, New York.

Editor's Note

Christopher Columbus mistakenly believed that the Antilles were the islands of the Indian Ocean, known to Europeans as the Indies, which he had hoped to reach by sailing west across the Atlantic. Even though Columbus's mistake was soon recognized, the name survived, and for centuries the native people of the Americas were either known by their tribal names or collectively called Indians.

More recently, many terms have been used to describe members of all tribes: Amerindians, Amerinds, First Americans, Original Americans, and Aboriginal or Indigenous Peoples. The term "Native American" was also introduced in the United States, initially by academics to avoid negative stereotypes thought to be associated with the term "Indian."

But the term "Native American" has also led to controversy. For example, Peter d'Errico, a consulting attorney on indigenous issues and emeritus professor of legal studies at the University of Massachusetts–Amherst, says the following about the term:

> "America" is derived from Amerigo Vespucci, a 16th century Italian navigator who was once said to be the "discoverer" of the continent. How can the people who were already here be named with his name?
>
> Other generic words are also seen to be problematic. "Native" and "indigenous" can rightfully be applied to anyone (or thing) born in a place, not only those who were arrived there born first. "Aboriginal"

> refers only to what was here "from the beginning," but the concept of "beginning" poses problems, too.
>
> Perhaps the best course is to refer to a People by the name they take for themselves. Sometimes this means using a word that means "we are the only true people," but at least it does not mean using a word that means "you are who others say you are."

Moreover, a 1995 US Census Bureau survey found that more descendants of the first settlers of what is now the United States preferred the term "American Indian" than the term "Native American." Russell Means, an American Indian activist, opposes the term Native American because he believes it was imposed by the government without the consent of American Indians. He has also argued that this use of the word Indian derives not from a confusion with India but refers to one of Columbus's diary entries in which he describes the natives as *una gente in Dios* ("a people in God").

In short, there is no universally agreed-upon term for the peoples—indeed, the sovereign nations—who lived and thrived before Columbus set foot on the North American continent. Moreoever, much of the book discusses their history before there even was an "America." In this edition of the book, therefore, you will see various terms used interchangeably: Indian, native peoples, early inhabitants, etc., though where possible we use the name each tribe used for itself.

—CRAIG R. SMITH

A typical Plains Indian village with the brightly decorated tepees of various clans: (left to right) Otter, Snow, Crow, and Snake. In the area at the top of the tepees the night sky is represented, showing the Big Dipper or the Indian emblem for the Morning Star, the Maltese Cross. In the center, you can see the religious design of the owner's family or a symbol of a great event in his tribal history. The band at the bottom is the earth, the peaked upper edge representing mountains or hills. The disks inside are "dusty stars," an Indian name for the puffballs growing in clusters on the plains.

Chapter One

The First Discoverers of the New World

When Columbus landed on a little island off the coast of Florida, he was not surprised to be met by what he termed Indians. For as far as he was concerned this was India and, while the natives might not have been as civilized as he had expected, they had to be Indians. Just as Columbus did not know that he would be given the title of discoverer of America, so he could not have known that the people he met were the distant descendants of the first discoverers of the New World who wandered over from Asia at least twenty-five thousand years earlier.

The historic blunder of Columbus wasn't long in being discovered, but the name "Indian" stuck. To most of the Spaniards who came after him one term was as good as another for the troublesome tribes they met. The Spaniards' eyes were fixed on gold and they were hardly interested in learning that the Indians—more than two thousand tribes in North America alone—had their own names for themselves. With the lure of treasure always just over the next hill, only an occasional priest stopped to observe the ways in which the Indians, through two hundred and fifty centuries of trial and error, had learned to live in harmony with each of the different environments across the vast continent.

When permanent European settlers came, however, the story was somewhat different. While their relations with the Indians were by no means always friendly, they were forced to study how their indigenous neighbors lived if they were to live in the wilderness themselves. It was corn from Indians, for example, that kept the Pilgrims alive through the winter after they landed in Massachusetts in 1620.

From that time on, the history of our country is inextricably tied up with the Indians. Trappers, explorers, pioneers, and missionaries found them in the woods and mountains, on the plains and deserts, and by the sea.

All over the country there were large distinct groups of Indians and within those groups were many tribes with different names and different customs and different languages. In Mexico Cortéz met the Aztecs; in Florida and the South De Soto met the Cherokee, the Choctaw, and the Creek; in the Southwest Coronado met some of the many Pueblo tribes; in Virginia the English dealt with the great chief Powhatan who ruled the Powhatan tribes, which spoke Algonquian. And in Massachusetts the Indian Squanto who befriended the Pilgrims belonged to another Algonquin tribe, the Wampanoag.

Squanto and Powhatan spoke languages that were related but distinct. In all, there were nearly three hundred different tongues spoken north of the Rio Grande, and at least half of these are still in use today. There was, however, no written language except in the advanced Mayan civilization.

Many native peoples, like the Mayans, were short and stocky. Others were tall and had high cheekbones and beaked noses, like the Sioux on our Indian nickel. Some had copper-colored skins, while others were very light and still others darker. None of the "redskins"were really red, of course. They came to be called so largely because many of them in Central and South America covered themselves with red paint for special occasions.

A young woman of one of the southern woodland tribes as she appeared to the Englishman John White more than three hundred and fifty years ago.

Although they called all the natives the newcomers met anywhere on the continent "Indians," each tribe thought of itself as unique and that its way of living was the right and natural way. The members of a tribe were likely to call themselves a name that meant "the real people" or "the original people" or just "the people." This was true of the Navaho in Arizona, of the Delaware in New Jersey, the Cheyenne in Colorado, and the Sioux in South Dakota as well as of almost all the Indian tribes.

Above left, a Chilkat chief from Alaska, in ceremonial dress, wears a hat that not only protects him from the rain but also tells to what family he belongs. The barefoot Seminole from Florida and the Cheyenne warrior (right) wear clothing of modern fabric and in styles that are a mixture of Indian and European. The gun came from white men. The spear resembles the earliest of Indian weapons. Like the Cheyenne, most Indians had little or no hair on their faces, but the Northwest Indians sometimes grew Chinese-style mustaches. The Seminole inherited the hair on his face from white or Negro ancestors.

The best way to learn about the colorful and dramatic histories and lives of the Indians is to take a look at the tribes in each of the large general groupings of Indians according to the area of the country in which they lived and the particular kind of life that adjusting to the plains, the deserts, the mountains, or the seacoast produced before the coming of the Europeans.

Woodland Indians used to inhabit the vast forests that covered much of the country from the Atlantic Ocean to the Mississippi River. Most of this forest is gone now. But four or five hundred years ago it was so dense that you would have thought there wasn't much room in it for people.

The Indians were not dismayed by all this forest. They turned the trees themselves into tools and weapons that helped them become masters of the woodlands. Some tribes made walls and roofs for their homes from big strips of bark. They used bark for the streamlined canoes in which they could bypass the tangles of the wilderness. Fish traps were built of young saplings driven into river bottoms and then laced together with tree branches. The hardwood trees of the forest made strong bows, reinforced with sinews from the animals that the bows helped to kill. Small boys learned to bend green twigs into ingenious traps and to prop up big logs as a deadfall in which to catch game. A teenage hunter was already so skilled in woodcraft that he could lure animals into shooting range by imitating their calls.

Woodland Indians were more than clever hunters, however. They were expert farmers, too.

So were many of the tribes west of the Mississippi. Here people built villages along the riverbanks and around the edges of the vast monotonous plains. Trees were few and far between. Grass, shoulder high in the east and shorter in the west, covered the land for hundreds of miles in every direction—a prison of grass. Once you entered it, you could not escape, for there were no landmarks to tell you where you were. Water was scarce, except in the infrequent rivers, and you could easily die of thirst. Nevertheless, native peoples succeeded in making the ocean of grass help them to live freely on its borders. Using the sod they walked on, they built homes that were cool in the intense summer heat and

An Indian of North Carolina in the 1580s. (After a drawing by John White, now in the British Museum.)

Most eastern woodland Indians lived in villages. They covered their houses with bark or bundles of grass or mats woven from reeds. For protection they built palisades of upright logs. The picture above shows how mat-covered houses on Roanoke Island off the coast of North Carolina looked to John White in 1585. White was governor of Sir Walter Raleigh's first colony there, and his drawings were the earliest known pictorial record of Indian life made by a European.

warm when blizzards swept down over the plains from the Arctic. They discovered that the heat of the sun, which made large chunks of meat decay, could also preserve meat that was cut into thin strips and hung up to dry.

For centuries, Plains Indians hunted the buffalo that grew fat on the endless pastures. But hunters who had to travel on foot could not make the swift animals their only source of food. They had to stay close to their sod-covered earth lodges and their cornfields. It was late in their history after the coming of the Spaniards that they were able to become horsemen and go wherever the buffalo went. Almost immediately they began to make the shaggy animals provide the movable shelter that hunters needed while they were following and killing the herds for food. Great skin tepees replaced the old earth lodges.

The dwellings of some Indian tribes were very simple, consisting of a framework of poles covered with brush and sometimes banked with earth in winter. This is a Miwok lodge in northern California.

In the Southwest, Indians made their homes on arid land where peculiar bristly plants grew from the clay soil. Bare ledges of sandstone jutted out of the earth, and deep canyons with cliff-wall sides slashed through the landscape. In early summer the sun baked the clay as hard as brick. By August torrential rains and flash floods ripped at the soil and carried much of it away. Such a land offered no easy living. But Indians managed to make even this thorny, barren place work for them. Fibers from the sharp yucca leaves became cloth. Yucca and spiny cactus fruits made delicious food. The hard clay soil proved to be good for growing corn, if the fields were planted and tended in the right way. Out of the sandstone rocks, people built homes that have lasted for hundreds of years.

These Pueblo Indians of the Southwest, who had such a battle against nature, were a peaceful people themselves. Still, they needed strong walls for protection against other tribes of wandering Indians who sometimes attacked them. The raiders, Navahos and Apaches, were hunters, who knew very little about getting a living in any other way. Since game animals were scarce in the Southwest, these newcomers often went hungry. Quite possibly they would have roamed in other directions if they had not discovered the well-fed Pueblo farmers whose storerooms held pottery jars full of corn.

At first the Navahos and Apaches tried to master the desert by stealing food from other people who had already learned how to live there. In the end they settled down to raise food of their own from the parched earth.

Still farther west, in what is now California and Nevada, the land was even more barren. No rains fell in summer, and no corn could grow. Here, too, Indians found a way of living. These people (we call some of them Diggers or Mission Indians) built homes of the brush that covered the brown hills. They discovered that they could eat certain roots and the seeds from wild plants. Along the seashore were clams and other seafood to be gathered and fish to be caught. Very few game animals lived in the area because green stuff was too scarce. Yet the Indians managed to exist because they learned to build their lives around the things that the land did offer.

A thousand miles north along the coast, the rain-soaked Northwest provided the material for an entirely different kind of life. Huge cedar trees grew straight and tall. Salmon clogged the rivers every spring. Here Indians made

The Shoshoni often lived in brush shelters until horses were brought to the Rocky Mountain area that was their hunting ground. Shoshonis then adopted from the horsemen of the Plains the easily movable skin-covered tepee.

the dripping forest and streams serve them well. They turned products of the rain into protection from rain. With shredded bark or reeds and grasses they fashioned hats and cloaks to keep them dry. Using tools of stone and bone, they split the great cedar trees into boards from which they built enormous community homes. They became expert carpenters and woodcarvers. But first of all they were fishermen. From the rivers they took thousands and thousands of salmon which they dried and hung from the rafters of their houses for year-round eating.

In the Far North, on the barren strip of land along the Arctic Ocean, still other people found a way to live without forests or farms, without even roots to dig or seeds to gather. They managed to feed themselves and to stay warm in some of the worst weather in all the world.

These people, the Eskimos, turned the animals and fish of their remote seacoast into weapons for conquering the frozen North. Where wood was

An Eskimo snow house, lined with an inner wall of animal skin, was as warm as a modern apartment. To build it, a man first cut blocks of snow with a special knife. Next, with his wife and children working outside, he stood inside and shaped the walls and dome, until the last block was laid. With his knife, he dug his way out, making a tunnel that became the entrance.

rare and too precious to burn, they got fuel—from seal oil. They even converted the killing snow of the long Arctic winters into a protection against snow, simply by building warm houses of it.

Within these general groupings were a bewildering variety of individual tribes. Yet, in spite of the great differences between them, they had many things in common. For example, the members of most tribes willingly shared whatever they had with each other. In the beginning, of course, they lived

Walpi, one of the Hopi pueblos. A snake dance is held here every other summer. As part of an elaborate rainmaking ritual, priests dance with live snakes in their mouths. Afterward the snakes are released to carry the Hopis' prayer for rain to the gods underground.

in small family groups and had to share their meat if the family was to survive. As groups grew larger, the habit continued and became a basic pattern of Indian life. Farmers worked together on land owned by the whole village. Every family had a portion of whatever corn there was. Hunters went out in groups, and after the hunt they made sure there was buffalo, rabbit, or antelope meat in each lodge. Very often several families shared one big dwelling.

The habit of sharing went beyond the family or village. If a stranger came to an Indian home, he was immediately offered food, and the hospitality continued as long as he appeared to have good intentions. This was true in the bark-covered longhouses of the Mohawks in New York and in the Pawnee earth lodges in Nebraska, in the great board dwellings of the Chinook on the west coast, in the apartment houses of the desert Hopi, and in the thatch-covered platforms that kept the Seminoles safe and dry above the swamps and alligators of Florida.

Almost all tribes living on or near the Great Plains held a buffalo dance to please the Buffalo Spirit who would bring good hunting. Often the dancers wore buffalo masks and imitated the motions of the great beasts as part of the ceremony.

In every tribe old people taught young people about the past and about the spirits that they believed were responsible for everything in their lives. They had stories and legends about the origin of the world and the way their own people came to live on the earth. Very often the legends explained how an individual family was descended from a particular animal. Because they were so dependent on it, Indians felt very close to all of nature and they were deeply respectful of the plants and animals they needed for their living.

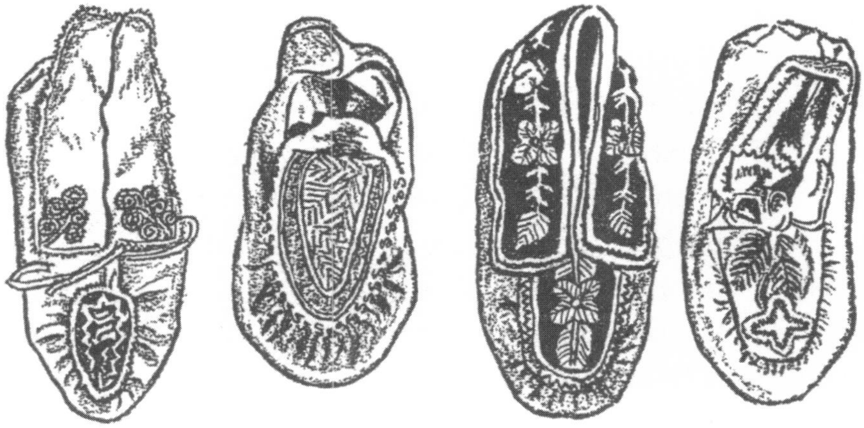

Moccasin styles varied from tribe to tribe. Some even had different styles for men and women. Usually women were the shoemakers. In many tribes they used colored porcupine quills for the decorations. Later they worked designs with colored beads they got from white traders.

As legends varied from tribe to tribe, they also had many similarities. For instance, Northwest Indians always put the bones of salmon back into the water. They believed that, since the fish had been polite enough to allow themselves to be caught, courtesy required that they allow the bones to return to the home of all salmon. Far off on the northeast coast, Algonquin Indians had the same custom. They never threw the bones of game animals to the dogs and they often hung the animals' skulls in trees to make it easier for their spirits to return to their home.

All native peoples had ceremonies, too—some very simple and some very elaborate—to please the spirits who brought good crops or the animals who would "allow themselves to be caught." These ceremonies were one of two ways by which Indians tried to control the world around them. First, they devised practical means—like their flint arrowheads or ingenious, detachable harpoon points—and then they developed rhythmic songs, dance steps, and prayers which they considered quite as effective as their weapons and tools.

Almost all Indian nations loved children and were very gentle and generous with them. Serious talks

Women of the eastern woodlands pounded hard kernels of corn into meal, using a hollowed-out stump for a mortar.

took the place of spankings. If a boy or a girl misbehaved, one of the older Indians explained the mistake. The shame of disapproval was a hard punishment; approval was a reward to be earned.

In most Indian tribes women had a highly respected place and they were responsible for as important a share of the work of the tribe as the men. Among woodland tribes, they grew the crops and cared for their homes, while the men hunted. In the Southwest, Pueblo men did not only the farming but the weaving as well. No matter how they divided the labor, however, women and men thought of themselves as equals.

As in every society all over the world since men first gathered together, every tribe had rules or customs to enable its people to get along with each other. There were very few hereditary rulers among the Indians inhabiting the area that is now the United States. Usually the members of a tribe selected their own chief whom they kept in office only as long as they approved of the job he was doing. For the most part, everyone had a voice in selecting a chief or in solving problems that arose every day from how to deal with marauding enemies to combating the deadly effect of a long drought. These elements of simple political democracy were apparent to those independent-minded white frontiersmen who lived peaceably among the Indians, and there is little doubt that what they saw played a part in their thinking when they set to work to establish a modern democracy of their own.

Wherever they were, native peoples studied the country around them and devised ways of getting along in it. Much of their development of plants for food was of enormous value to those who came after them. First, and most important, they introduced corn to the rest of the world—three hundred varieties of it. From the earliest days of white immigration this grain has been of utmost importance until today it is the most valuable crop in the whole country.

Spaniards landing in Latin America found corn, recognized its value, and appropriated it. It was corn that saved the lives of Captain John Smith's company at Jamestown in 1609 and of the Pilgrims at Plymouth ten

Eastern woodland Indians collected the sap of the Sugar-Maple tree in bark pots. With a bark ladle they dipped hot syrup from the boiling kettle and poured it on the snow to cool and harden into candy.

years later. Smith's method of "borrowing" corn from his new neighbors was very simple and direct.

Loading a boat with men carrying muskets, he rowed to an Indian village and started shooting when the inhabitants showed signs of reluctance to part with their food supply. Then he offered to make peace if they filled his boat with the precious grain.

The Pilgrims' method was not very different. On their first day on land they explored the beach at Cape Cod and found buried in the sand a large basket which, their historian noted, was "very handsomely and cunningly made." It held corn, "some in eares, faire and good, of diverce colours, which seemed to them a very goodly sight (having never seen any before)." So good, in fact, did the corn seem that the pious Pilgrims assigned a guard to protect them from the Indians while they filled their pockets and a large kettle with the promising addition to their diet.

A wigwam (left) and a tepee (right), drawn side by side to show their difference. Wigwams were characteristic of many eastern woodland people, but some of them used the bark-covered tepee. When they moved to the plains, they took the tepee idea with them, substituting buffalo skins for bark.

Having corn was all well and good, but the inexperienced Englishmen at Plymouth could only eat it. They had no idea how to grow more. For this knowledge they were dependent on Squanto, the English-speaking Wampanoag, who taught them the mysteries of planting and cultivating the seeds in hills, using fish as fertilizer.

Essential though it was, corn merely led a long list of foods that white men took over from the Indians. White ("Irish") potatoes, sweet potatoes, peanuts, turkeys, tomatoes, cocoa, pineapple, strawberries, artichokes, most kinds of beans, chili peppers, many varieties of squash, pumpkins, maple syrup and sugar—these were some of them. In addition, we are fond of Indian recipes, such as succotash, tamales, hominy, mush, barbecued meat, and the whole clambake menu.

Tobacco, of course, came from the Indians, together with the practice of smoking it. There were important native drugs like quinine, cocaine, cascara sagrada, oil of wintergreen, ipecac, witch hazel, and arnica. Although scientists did not get the idea of penicillin from the Indians, many South American people discovered, no one knows how long ago, that a wound dressed with a certain kind of fungus healed cleanly. Penicillin is a product of that fungus.

Indians were the first people to discover and put rubber to use and they invented hammocks, toboggans, and snowshoes. White pioneers moving west in the wilderness could not have survived without their knowledge of Indian woodcraft. They wore moccasins and buckskin leggings and shirts. They built wigwams, tepees, and sod houses of their own, and they always followed Indian trails. As the number of pioneers increased, the trails widened so that horses and then ox carts and covered wagons could follow them. Railroads came and followed the wagon roads. To this day many stretches of the Pennsylvania line, for instance, follow old Indian trails in the Alleghenies. Modern highways, such as the Mohawk Trail in New York, make the turns and twists they do because long ago Indians discovered that the route they follow was the best.

Every day of our lives we use words, phrases, or names of Indian origin: chipmunk, woodchuck, Indian file, hominy, skunk, going on the warpath, burying the hatchet, smoking the peace pipe, Pontiac, Tammany. At least five hundred Indian words are part of everyday English. Nearly half of our states have Indian names, and so do thousands of rivers, mountains, cities, and counties. In summer camps children become familiar with Indian lore and woodcraft, as do the Boy Scouts and Girl Guides. In fact, a Dakota (Santee Sioux), Charles Eastman, was a founder of the Boy Scout movement.

Animals like the mastodon and the hairy mammoth (above) and the ground sloth (next page), which are now extinct, roamed over much of North America when the first Indians arrived.

Chapter Two

Where Did Indians Come From?

THROUGHOUT MOST OF man's long life on this earth there was not a single human being in all of North and South America. Wildlife flourished, but so far as people were concerned these two continents were a huge vacuum. And then between twenty-five and thirty thousand years ago men began to trickle in through a small opening.

For a million years, the ancestors of these first immigrants had lived through the Ice Age in the eastern half of the world. During that time, great sheets of ice periodically shoved and ground their way down from the Arctic over much of Europe, Siberia, and North America. Game animals retreated before the ice. Men, who ate meat when they could get it, followed the game. The world in those days wasn't nearly as cold as you might think, and a great deal of plant life grew near the edges of the glaciers. This meant that animals lived close to the fringes of the icecap, and so did man.

All of the water that was frozen in the glaciers, sometimes ten thousand feet thick, had evaporated from the oceans and then had fallen as snow. Consequently, the level of the oceans was lower than it is today—three hundred feet lower in some places—and land stood out where none can now be seen.

The fifty-six-mile stretch between Siberia and Alaska was one such place. Curiously, the snow fell much less heavily there than on the great landmasses, and the coasts of Alaska and Canada, too, were free of ice long before the glaciers melted and disappeared from other regions. Animals began to wander across the land bridge between the two continents, then south along the ice-free American shoreline. And men, always on the lookout for good hunting, trailed the animals. And so it was that twenty-five thousand years ago—more or less—men first came to America.

In the new world they found better hunting than they had ever dreamed of. Nobody had been there ahead of them, and native game of all kinds roamed everywhere. Scientists have estimated that, in any one season at that time, a wildlife census of America would have shown forty million of the largest game animals that have ever lived.

These pioneers did not face the wilderness entirely naked and empty-handed. They brought along a few important tools and weapons that they had perfected slowly—very slowly—and they were masters of the knowledge their far off ancestors had collected in at least a million years of very tough existence. They had learned to use spears and to do the delicate work of shaping flint to make spear points. They carried a tricky gadget we call a spear-thrower or atl-atl, which made it possible for a man to hurl his spear three times as hard and three times as far as he could with his bare hand.

The earliest inhabitants of this continent also had curved, flat, bladelike sticks that they could aim accurately at rabbits and other small game. They knew how to grind up edible seeds by putting them on a flat rock and rubbing another rock over them. In cold weather they wrapped themselves in animal skins and they knew how to build campfires as well—for warmth and maybe even for the good flavor that cooking gave to meat. Possibly they had learned

Very often the early Indian used a spear-throwing device that, acting like an extra joint to his arm, gave him greatly increased power.

to make baskets out of grass or reeds or shreds of bark, and they may have brought along dogs. A dog could carry a small burden on his back, and a family could eat him in time of need.

For the most part, however, no one needed dog meat in the new land. It was a hunter's paradise. Huge red-brown hairy mammoths roamed everywhere, trumpeting and swinging their great curled tusks at bothersome creatures like saber-toothed tigers. They never lacked for leaves and twigs to eat, and men who knew the trick of killing them never lacked for mammoth steak.

Spears, even with spear-throwers, were not much use against these animals' tough hides. The surest thing was to frighten them and drive them over a cliff or into a swamp. Humans had what it took to scare a mammoth—fire. A grass or forest fire, planned in advance to burn at the right place, would send the lumbering creatures off in a panic over the edge of a precipice. The same trick worked for other big game—and much of the game was big. Elk, deer, buffalo, and beaver were all larger than they are now, and elephants we call mastodons roamed the country along with their hairy cousins, the mammoths.

The woods and plains of the new world were filled with many animals that are now extinct, possibly killed off by the wasteful prairie- and forest-fire method of hunting. Here and there giant sloths clumped along on the backsides of their front paws because their curved claws were so long they could not get the soles of their feet on the ground. Small camels were abundant, as were swift-running, big-bellied horses. These horses were native to America

Very often the early Indian used a spear-throwing device that, acting like an extra joint to his arm, gave him greatly increased power.

and, since there was two-way traffic over the land bridge between Alaska and Siberia, they wandered into Asia. There they remained and became the ancestors of modern horses, long after the original American variety had died out. The newcomers fed on all these animals.

After a while, as they moved southward along the edges of the glaciers, groups of people began to branch out from the main stream of the migration. Some spread out to the southeast into country that the great ice sheets hadn't touched. Others pushed on through Mexico and into South America.

Behind them more and more hunters kept coming. At the same time the glaciers were slowly retreating. About fifteen thousand years ago the ice had melted back far enough so that a new route opened up. Groups could follow the Yukon River and cross a low pass to the Mackenzie River. From there it was fairly easy going over ice-free country all the way through Canada

Among the animals the first Indians found were camels and horses, but both died out thousands of years before the Spaniards re-introduced horses from Europe.

and onto the Great Plains east of the Rockies. Wave after wave of people followed this route. Latecomers fought with older inhabitants for the right to hunt, but they mingled with each other, too, and wandered farther, until at last there were human beings all over the Americas.

These migrations went on even after the ocean rose and covered the fifty-six miles between Siberia and Alaska. Some bands of people may have walked

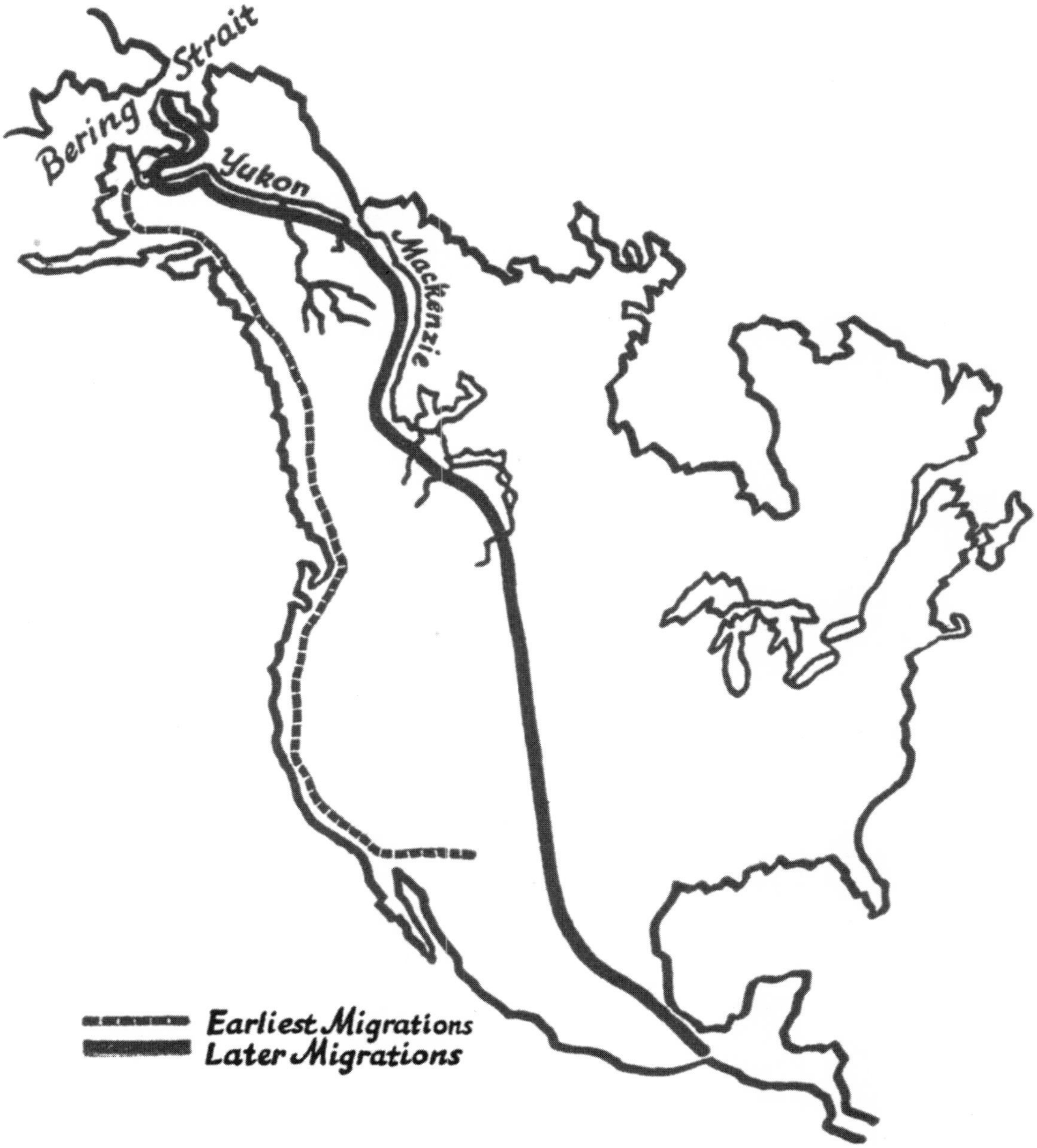

across the ice-covered Bering Strait in winter, and others probably came in the skin boats they had learned to make. New groups kept arriving, bringing with them new inventions and ideas, up until a few hundred years before Christ.

The experts on Indian history generally agree that this is about the way things happened. But there are some who believe that an additional group of settlers followed still another route not long before the Christian era. It is possible, they say, that large ocean-going canoes with sails brought people across the Pacific to the coast of Central and South America. Such a theory is tempting, because it explains the very strong similarities between Indian life in those areas and the life of people on the Pacific islands, in India, and even in Asia Minor. On the other hand, there is the theory, put to the test and somewhat borne out by the Dane Thor Heyerdahl and his companions in their famous voyage on the raft *Kon-Tiki,* that some of the South Sea peoples originally came from the western shores of South America. But, until more evidence turns up, both theories remain to be proved.

Since most of the Indians came to America by way of Siberia, you might naturally jump to the conclusion that they were Mongolian, that perhaps they resembled the Chinese. Many of them did, but not the earliest arrivals. They had in them very different strains which are now found among peoples in distant areas of the earth.

In the days when a land bridge connected Alaska with Siberia, people were already traveling on foot all over the ice-free parts of Asia, Europe, and Africa. As they wandered, they met and mingled with other peoples. So it was a great mixture of people who made the long journey through the gateway to America. How do we know all this? Since this was before the time of recorded history, there was no one to describe the immigrants as they trudged into Alaska, barefoot or in crude sandals or as they pulled their simple gear out of skin canoes. Still, we know the rough outlines of their story because each group left telltale clues to the way they looked, the way they lived, the routes they followed.

Every wandering band stopped and camped from time to time. This meant that they left ashes and garbage, and they lost things around camp, just as people still do. Since caves offered the best shelter, any conspicuous cavern was bound to attract more than one group. Each left its debris on top of the remains from other camps, in layer after layer. Other bands stopped beside rivers where shifting currents and floods covered the sites with mud and sand. Some camped on the prairies by lakes that have long since dried up. Grass grew over the refuse, gradually forming earth which protected many clues to ancient life.

Archeologists have dug patiently and carefully through hundreds of these campsites. Obviously, the newest debris will be at the top of any site that was used many times. Slicing down through the layers, the scientists look for anything, no matter how tiny, that may be connected with man—a stone that has been chipped, a fragment of a clay bowl, a bone shaped into an awl, points for spears or arrows, even pieces of charcoal. As they dig, they make minute records of everything they find. Then they compare the findings from one campsite with findings from many others. Suppose they discover, in addition to human remains, a lot of huge bison bones and some straight horns in one layer of earth. Since modern buffalo always have curved horns, the hunters who camped here must have lived before the giant bison died out. Paleontologists—students of ancient animal life—can tell approximately when the big animals became extinct. Thus, we have an approximate date for this particular layer of human debris.

Professional diggers aren't the only ones who have done detective work on the history of America's first people. Some of the most important finds were made by cowboys.

One cold December day in 1889, a young cowpoke named Richard Wetherill was looking for stray cattle among the juniper and piñon trees on the high, flat top of Mesa Verde in southwestern Colorado. At an open spot he paused on the rim of one of the many canyons that gash deep into the mesa. Below him was a sheer cliff dropping hundreds of feet to the canyon bottom, and across on the other side rose another cliff wall. All the canyons were like that, but suddenly Wetherill noticed something different here—a shallow cave high in the opposite canyon wall, and in the cave was a large building. He couldn't believe his eyes.

Wetherill investigated. The building really was there—a sort of apartment house with many rooms, and in the rooms he found clay pots with intricate designs worked in gray and black.

The cowboy had stumbled on the remains of a civilization nobody knew existed. His curiosity was greatly roused. He explored the canyons and found more ruins, littered with tools, clothing, utensils, even the mummylike remains of former residents whose bodies had simply dried out in the

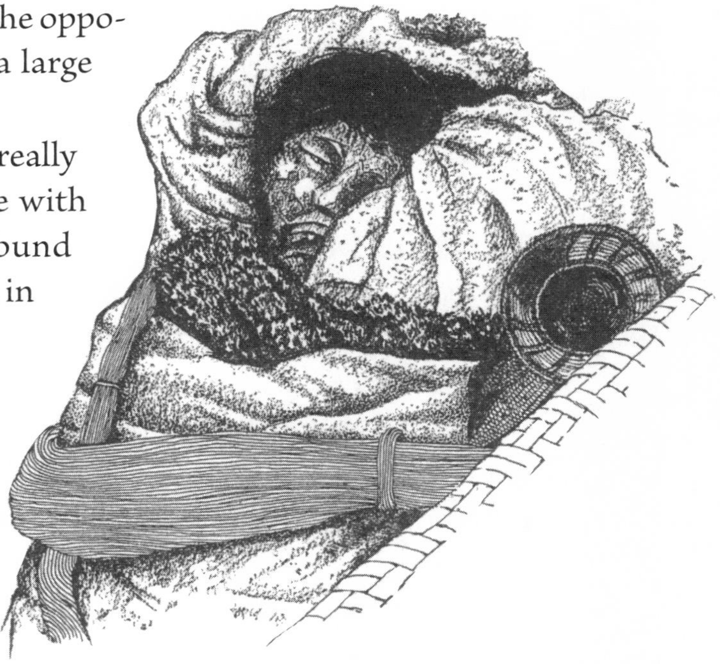

Cliff dwellers sometimes sealed the bodies of the dead in rooms of their houses, where the dry southwestern air preserved them. This mummy-like body, now in the American Museum of Natural History in New York, is wrapped in a turkey feather blanket with hundreds of yards of cotton yarn.

desert air. Before long, Richard Wetherill became a real expert on ancient Indian life and he was much respected by archeologists from universities and museums, except for one thing: he financed his explorations by selling the beautiful old pots and other relics that he found. Many of his discoveries were thus lost to science, but enough remained so that archeologists could put together a picture of a people who lived long before any written history in this country.

Another cowboy, an African American named George McJunkin, also turned up material of great importance in northern New Mexico. His discovery led to the realization that people had lived here several thousand years earlier than any scientist had ever been able to prove before.

McJunkin had been riding range one chilly day in 1926. Toward evening he looked across a deep arroyo and saw something that looked like a lot of bones sticking out of the earth. Although cowboys in general don't like to walk, and this particular cowboy was tired, he decided to have a closer look. The location of the bones showed that they had been buried under twelve feet of soil. McJunkin realized they must be very old indeed to lie so far below the surface. The bones were unlike, any he had ever seen before. Moreover, his knife turned up two flint spear points that did not at all resemble the points that he occasionally picked up around old Ute or Apache campsites.

Later, in the nearby village of Folsom, the cowboy spread the word of his curious find. It wasn't long before a scientist in Colorado heard the news and came down for a look at the bones. He found that they had belonged to the extinct giant bison with the long straight horns. The delicately chipped flint points were unlike any that had ever been found before—they had long grooves down the middle of each side. And they lay among the bones in such a way that it seemed certain they had killed the big beasts.

Other scientists came and dug out more bones and spear points. They noticed one additional curious fact. Most of the buffalo skeletons were complete, except for the tailbones. The hunters who killed the animals had not carved them up for meat. Instead, they had skinned them, tail and all, just the way later Indians did. This could only mean that the unknown people had some use for skins, very probably as clothing.

The earth above the bones gave another clue. Geologists estimated that it must have taken ten thousand years to pile up a twelve-foot layer here. It is known that the giant bison have been extinct for nearly ten thousand years.

Therefore, the men whose spear points were embedded in the bison must have lived about ten thousand years ago.

This one find left many unanswered questions: Had the spear points been made by a distinct group of people, whom we call Folsom men after the town close by? If so, who were they? Where did they come from? A gold miner added a clue that indicated some partial answers. He found a Folsom spear point in Alaska, and scientists following after him found more of them. Other points turned up east of the Rocky Mountains. It looked very much as if Folsom men had come from Siberia, across Alaska, then down through Canada onto the Great Plains.

For some years Folsom man was considered the oldest inhabitant of America. Then one day a college student discovered an unexplored cave in the Sandia Mountains near Albuquerque, New Mexico. He led archeologists to the spot, and as they crawled back into the hole, dodging bats, they found the claw of a giant sloth, an animal long extinct. That was interesting in itself, but the floor of the cave gave the scientists their real reward. They dug down, hunting for ancient human remains, and found them in layer after layer. Here, for thousands of years off and on, men had built cooking fires and left animal bones and bits of the things they used for tools. Near the bottom of the heap were traces of Folsom man. And below that were crude spear points, quite different from Folsom points and thousands of years older.

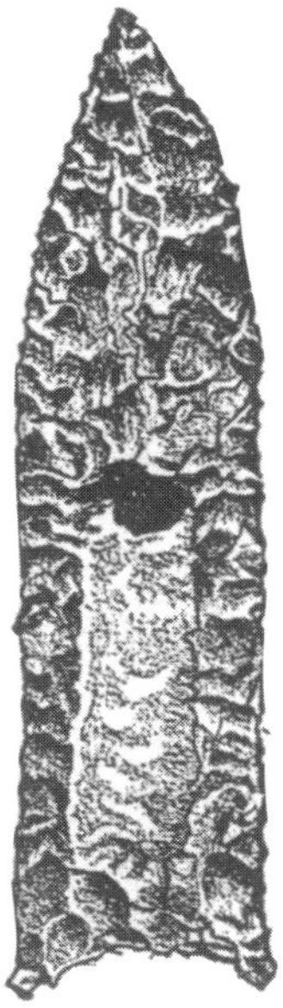

All over the country, farmers, construction workers, Boy Scouts, people of many kinds have dug and found stone implements and bones. Scientists, crouched on their knees, have scratched carefully with trowels and swept away dust with camel's-hair brushes, looking for evidence of man's past. Then they have studied their finds in laboratories with microscopes and chemical tests. Atomic science has helped them to determine accurate dates for bits of charcoal from ancient campfires.

In the Southwest, dates have been fixed by studying the growth of tree rings. Each year of its life a tree adds a new ring of wood under the bark—thick ones in wet years, thin ones in times of drought. By matching one set of rings from a tree known to have been cut in a certain year, against rings from trees whose ages

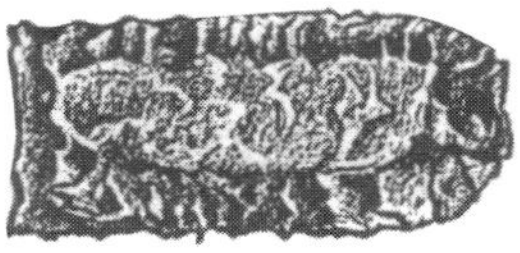

The delicately shaped spear points made by Folsom men always have a groove down the middle of each side.

were unknown, scientists have gradually pieced together a chart of rings going back to CE 11. By matching any cross section of wood against the master chart of tree rings, they can tell the year a tree was cut down. With this method of dating the wooden beams in the ruins of Southwest Indian houses, we know almost the exact year any building was put up.

Other scientists have measured human skulls and skeletons. They have examined the bumps and ridges on bones to find the shape and size of ancient men's muscles. Gradually they have built up a picture of what Indians looked like long ago, and every year brings new discoveries.

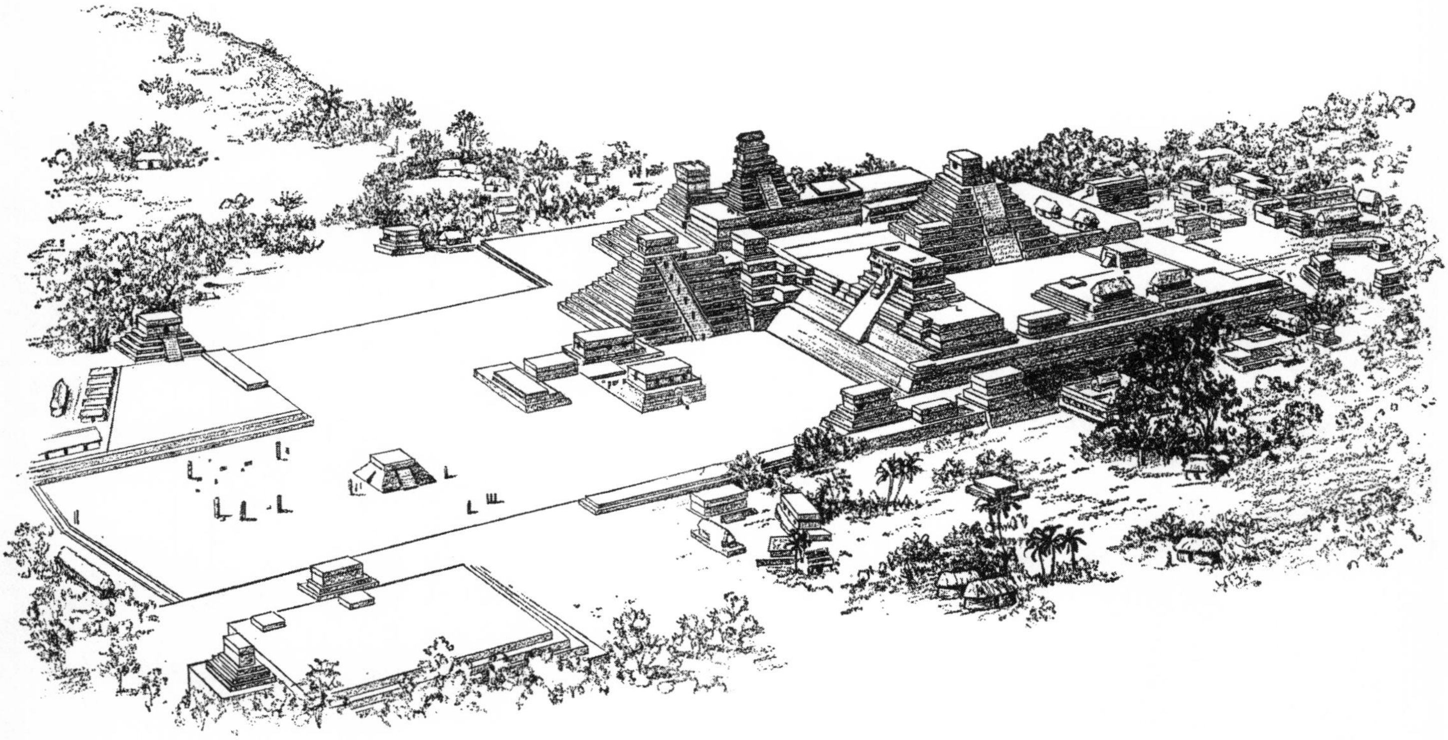

The great temples and public buildings of the Mayan city of Copan,
from a reconstruction drawing by Tatiana Proskouriakoff.

Chapter Three

The Mayan Miracle

FOR THOUSANDS OF years Indians explored the steaming lowland jungles and the cooler highlands of Central and South America. They lived on the wild animals they downed with slings, spears, and blowguns and on plants, fruits, and seeds. Then, about five thousand years ago, somewhere in Central America or northern South America, they made a discovery that was to have far-reaching results.

They found a wild grass with large pods of seeds that could be used for food. Each seed was wrapped in its own separate husk. In itself this find was not unusual. Indians had been discovering new food seeds wherever they went. But this time, someone—probably a woman since women did the cooking and much of the food gathering—hit upon the idea that the seeds would produce new plants year after year if they were planted in the ground. Instead of searching around for patches of wild grain, she could have seedpods to gather right where she wanted them, close to a good campsite.

This unknown woman founded agriculture for the Americas. Later, other women discovered that if they sowed seeds from the biggest pods they got better crops. In this way, season after season for hundreds of years they improved the yield from the grass that had once grown wild. Cultivation of the grass spread among the Indians. Then someone happened to sow these seeds near a stand of a different kind of grass called teosinte. Pollen

was carried from one field to the other. From this cross-pollination came seeds with new traits. Some produced plants that had many more seeds in each head of grain. A harvest from such seeds could feed more people than before.

As time passed, freak seeds appeared on the stalks. In some of the freaks many kernels of grain grew together in a bunch, with one husk wrapped around them all. Since it was much easier to get the husks off such ears of grain, Indian women saved and planted some of the kernels, which produced more of the new kind of ear. Indians had changed the wild grass into the plant we call corn—or maize from the name the Spaniards derived from a Caribbean language.

These stylized pictures of corn were made by Aztecs, the military conquerors who came after the Mayans.

Corn, in turn, changed human life. Men joined their wives in planting and harvesting. This was very different from the old hunting days when the men had to spend most of their time out in the forest. There was a much steadier and bigger food supply now that they put part of their energies into farming. Before long so much food came from the farms that many people could specialize in other work. With time free from the uncertainties and drudgery of hunting for all their food, they found more and more ways of being creative.

One of the groups of indigenous peoples who so profited from the growth of corn were the Mayans in Central America. Very quickly these Indians developed a great civilization in what had once been wilderness. Even today scholars disagree about the source of the Mayans' ideas. There seems to be some evidence that strangers familiar with much of the learning of India and the Near East crossed the Pacific by way of the South Sea Islands and settled in Central America. Perhaps they taught the Mayans the things they had known in the Orient. Whatever may have been the reasons, however, the Mayans had a culture as brilliant and as rich as that of ancient Egypt. We can get a pretty good idea of Mayan life at its height if we look in on a typical Mayan city about the year 1000 CE.

The morning sun beats down on the temples and palaces of this huge city. In the paved streets and over in the huge plaza, which is the center of activity, tens of thousands of people are milling about laughing and talking. Most of the people are farmers and this is a great day for them, for they usually get to the city only for such religious holidays as this one and they never tire of marveling at the sights it has to offer.

Unlike the tall people of the woodlands with whom we are more familiar, these Mayans are short and stocky. Most of them have foreheads sloping straight back to a peak, so that their heads seem cone-shaped, and many are cross-eyed. These deformities are fashionable. A mother straps her baby's head between two boards when the bones are still soft, and the pressure molds it into a peak.* She hangs a toy close to his face so that he will grow up with crossed eyes.

Many of these Mayans are wearing cotton mantles, but others are in everyday dress, which is only a breechcloth for men and a long skirt for the few women who have come out. Others will join the crowd when they have finished their daily chore of grinding corn between two stones and then cooking flat pancakes and tamales for the family. The faces of all the married men are painted red. The boys and unmarried men have their faces covered with black.

Militia men have put on their gay three-inch-thick quilted cotton armor. Their tall helmets, decorated with brilliant feathers from tropical birds, stand high above the throng. At their sides hang short wooden swords with blades made of razor-sharp bits of black volcanic glass.

Priests, painted black all over and dressed in jaguar skins, busy themselves near the temples—those enormous stone buildings reaching skyward from great pyramids of earth which are completely covered with smooth stone and cement. Hundreds of stone steps lead up each pyramid to the dazzling temple on top. Carvings decorate the whole building. Some are portraits of important people. Many represent animals, often strange imaginary creatures. One of these is the sacred Feathered Serpent, the emblem of the great god of creation, Kukulcan, who was half bird and half snake. Another is of a youth wearing a headdress of leaves, and this is the all-important

This typical intricate Mayan design represents the Feathered Serpent, an important god.

* Editor's note: See page 121 for an illustration of this practice.

Maize God or Lord of the Harvest. All the carvings are painted brilliant colors—yellow, red, green, blue, white.

Color is everywhere. Noblemen wear bright, embroidered cloaks. Some of them ride impressively through the crowd in decorated litters carried by their servants. The common people look up curiously. One noble has jewelry of gold, silver, and turquoise dangling from his ears and nose. Another wears his in a hole pierced through his lower lip. If he happens to smile, there is a flash of color from the jewels set in his teeth.

A Mayan man of importance sits on a throne surrounded by nobles.
(Drawn from an elaborate sculpture found at Piedras Negras, Guatemala.)

Shoppers wander among the market stalls where everything imaginable is for sale—strips of cotton cloth, copper bells to be worn as ornaments, sharp knives chipped from the same natural black glass called obsidian that the militia men use in their swords. Bright feathers from tropical birds are for sale in one shop; curiously shaped pots covered with intricate designs are in another. In food stalls are avocados, chili peppers, little hairless dogs, breadfruit, the delicious tails of iguana lizards, honey which farmers have gathered from their hives of stingless bees, and the meat of wild boars. Any of these things and hundreds of others can be bought for the cocoa beans that everyone uses as money.

Country people, enjoying the sights of the city, stop now and then to wonder at the tall columns of solid stone placed here and there along the streets. Elaborate carvings cover every square inch of the columns, telling the history of the Mayans and giving the exact dates of important events. Very few of the passersby can read the message. Only the priests can read.

A crowd, tense with excitement, fills the stone grandstands around the big basketball court near the largest temples. Two teams of seven players struggle with each other to score a goal with a big solid live-rubber ball. Just one goal wins the game, and for a good reason. The two stone hoops are eighteen feet above the stone floor of the court, sticking out at right angles to the position of the hoops used in basketball today. A player may not use his hands to get the ball through a hoop. He can only bounce it off his shoulders, hips, arms, or head. It takes a long time to make that one goal.

The nobles, who sit in the best seats, all look as if they are getting ready to leave—and they are. At any moment they may start scrambling out of the grandstand, for according to the rules of the game the player who makes a basket may climb into the stand and claim any pieces of jewelry or clothing he can lay his hands on.

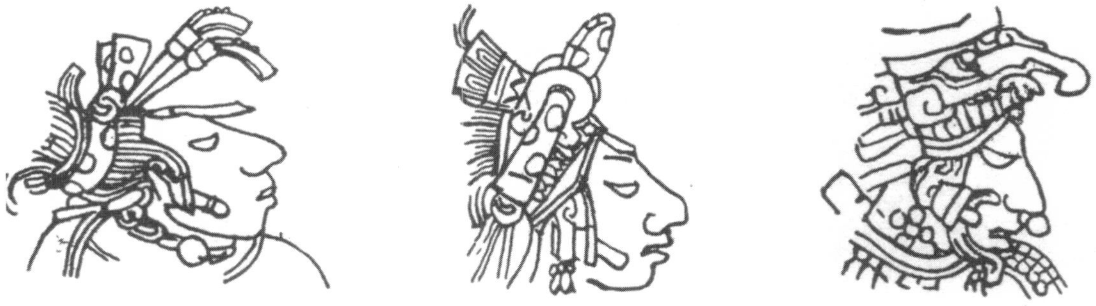

These profiles are drawn from Mayan sculpture and show typically flattened foreheads.

Everywhere you look you can see signs of the ingenuity of the Mayan craftsmen. Around the plaza are palaces, some of them three stories high, belonging to the nobles and the priests. All are built of stone perfectly shaped by masons who had only stone tools with which to work. Under the streets run sewers made of stone and cement. Where the city streets end, paved roadways continue on for miles out into the country. Religious pilgrims walk along these highways from their homes to the gleaming temples.

All of these roads and streets, basketball courts, pyramids, and temples have obviously been built according to a careful plan. But there seems to be less plan in the city as you move away from the plaza. Beyond the palaces and temples cluster simple houses made of woven sticks plastered over with mud and roofed with palm leaves. Here the common people live, the people who do the enormous labor of digging, hauling, and lifting that is needed to erect the magnificence of pyramids and palaces.

Beyond the city, more such simple houses are scattered for miles over the countryside, up to the very edge of the jungle. Great fields stretch out in every direction. Here live the families who raise food for the city dwellers. The farmers seem to grow weeds and crops in about equal quantities. They do not cultivate the land. They simply plant their corn and other seeds and let anything grow that will in the warm tropical climate.

Ancient Mayan farmers lived in thatched huts, and their descendants still use this kind of dwelling today.

Other things seem strange, too, in a country where so many farmers plant and harvest crops. They have not one single tool made of iron. There are no farm animals except turkeys and dogs—no cattle, no sheep, goats, or hogs, no horses to carry heavy burdens of food to the city. People have to take everything on their own backs or in canoes.

They don't even have carts they can push along. No one in America has yet discovered how to use wheels to make work easier.

Far off in the distance, beyond the city and across thick stretches of jungle, lie other cities and towns and villages, all with their pyramids, temples, and beautiful art.

A Mayan farmer always carried a drinking gourd filled with water when he went to work.

This was the land of the Maya Indians who lived over a thousand years ago in Honduras, Guatemala, and the part of southern Mexico called Yucatan.

A closer look at the Mayans would have shown other amazing achievements—all made possible by the leisure and wealth that developed from the cultivation of corn. The key to many of these achievements was astronomy.

With abundant food some men could devote all their time to being priests and making the magic that people thought would help the crops. Priests made offerings and said prayers to the sun, the moon, and the stars, for it was from the heavens that the life-giving rain came. As they looked toward the

Mayans often decorated their pottery with pictures of people.

sky they noticed that the heavenly bodies moved in regular ways and they linked these movements with the seasons. Finally they found out how to tell almost exactly when the rainy season was due. This was vitally important to the farmers, who needed to get their corn plants well rooted before the coming of the violent rains which were likely to wash the seeds out of the soil.

A Toltec doll.

To keep a record of the movements of the stars, the sun, and the moon, two other things were essential. First of all, the priests needed arithmetic in order to do their calculations about the stars, and they needed a way of writing so they could preserve their findings. The Mayans developed both.

Now a calendar could be kept, and the Mayans made one that was more accurate than any in the world at that time. Indeed, it was as accurate as our calendar today. Experimenting with numbers, they invented the idea of zero a thousand years before anyone in any other part of the world had done so.

As their knowledge of arithmetic grew, the priests found they could use it for many things besides calculating when the rains would come. Since they could now measure accurately, they could design large buildings. Thus, they became architects.

This is the Aztec calendar. It was based on the Mayan calendar which was as accurate as the one we use today.

In their leisure time they could think up ways of preserving their knowledge. The most lasting record, of course, is one carved on stone. So enormous blocks of stone were quarried by Mayan laborers, and every five years the priests had them shaped into columns, which were then carved all over with symbols, or glyphs, spelling out their history. They also invented bark paper, on which they wrote or figured out astronomy problems. They even made a start toward printing by cutting glyphs in reverse on hard material the way modern printer's type is made. When the glyph was painted with dye and pressed against paper it left its stamp.

Not all of the priests' inventions were so practical, however. They advanced from telling people when to plant to telling them when to do everything else. Astronomers turned astrologers and gave advice on everything from when

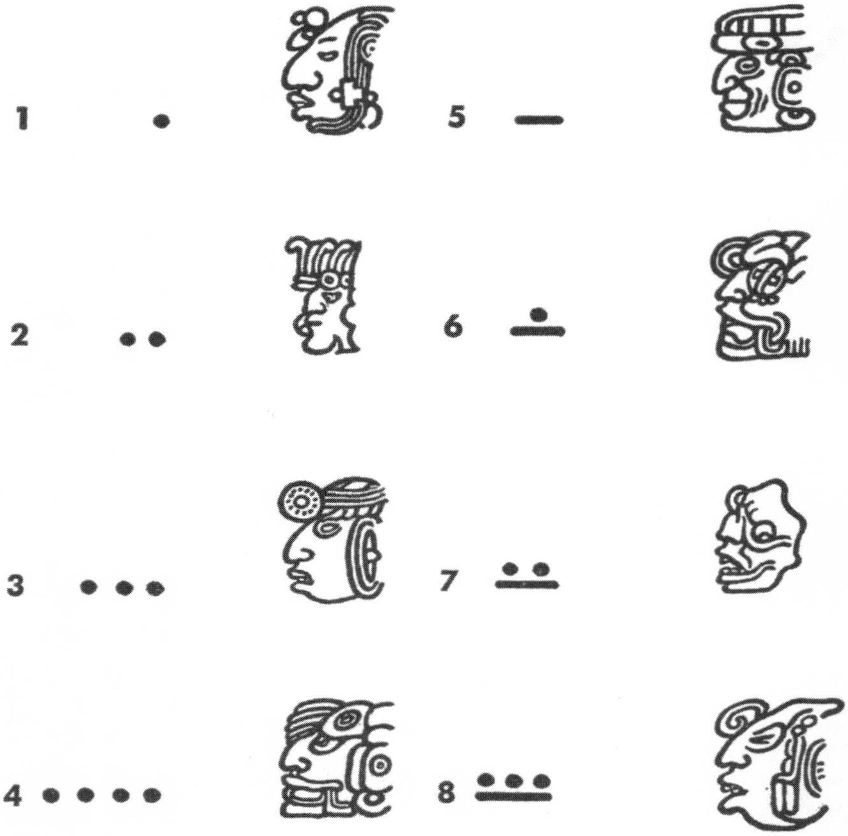

Mayans wrote numbers in two different ways just as we use both numerals (1, 2, 3, etc.) and words (one, two, three, etc.). Mayan numerals were a combination of dots and dashes. They wrote their words in symbols which we call glyphs.

to marry to when to build temples. They had elaborate systems of lucky and unlucky days. For their very real ability to make predictions about the stars they won respect, but as they grew wealthy and powerful, they used pseudo-science to keep the illiterate farmers in a state of fear and obedience.

In every city the priests became the real rulers. They had charge of the peacetime life of the whole people. Beside them a class of nobles grew up in luxury. From among the nobles came the war leader, in charge of the

More Mayan numerical glyphs.

volunteer militia who protected each city. During most of Mayan history these war leaders were not as important as the priests, for the Mayans were a peaceful people.

Perhaps to increase the ordinary man's awe of them, the priests developed a theory that human beings should be sacrificed to the gods.

The gods, they explained, were pleased when people returned to the earth some of the things that the earth had generously given to man. Offerings of food were valuable, but the people who grew it were more so. It seemed logical that the gods would be especially pleased if human blood, or human life itself, was returned to the earth. So in times when crops failed and the gods seemed angry, the lives of handsome young men or women slaves, captives from enemy tribes, were offered to appease them. It was a high honor to be selected for sacrifice, and the victim's every wish was granted before the fateful day when a priest would stretch him on an altar and cut his living heart out of his body.

Bloody and cruel though human sacrifice seems to us, it had a deep religious meaning to the Mayans. As time went on, they did more and more of it. For one thing, there were more and more slaves to be sacrificed—captives taken in wars that plagued the Mayan cities toward the end of their history. Efforts were made to form a strong league of the various cities as protection against primitive tribes that came to steal their wealth, but jealousy among the war leaders kept them from cooperating. Civil war broke out. Soon afterward the jungle moved in and covered over the great cities. Even before the Spaniard Cortéz invaded Mexico in 1519, the rich Mayan civilization was a thing of the past, although Mayans themselves still live in Mexico and parts of Central America.

After the Mayan civilization had ended, Aztecs conquered much of Mexico. They, too, built great temples in which they carried human sacrifice to much greater extremes than the Mayans ever had. This Aztec drawing shows a priest cutting out the victim's heart with a stone knife.

During the hundreds of years it flourished, news of the brilliant Mayan world traveled far and wide. It was carried largely by the Mayans themselves for they were always on the move.

Strange as it seems, these people who had developed corn and then built a great civilization, often had to move because they did not have enough to eat. Their crops would fail, and neither they nor their learned priests figured out why. The men who had made the wonderfully accurate observations and done the mathematics needed for their calendar never discovered the simplest facts about soil conservation.

The earth of the jungle floor was thin. As long as trees grew there, the roots kept it from washing away. But when trees were killed to make room for crops, tropical rains carried soil down into the rivers. Even when fields were not washed away, many of the minerals that nourished corn plants disappeared from the soil in a few years. Still, no one dreamed of building dams

Warriors from other peoples—perhaps Toltecs like this chief casting his spear at two Mayan warriors who are trying to escape—conquered many Mayan cities and borrowed much of Mayan civilization. (From a Toltec disk of gold.)

or of fertilizing or rotating crops. Naturally the land wore out. The farmers had to move farther and farther from the cities in order to find a place where corn would grow. Finally, they got so far from their markets that the cities themselves had to move. People simply abandoned the vast pyramids, temples, and palaces and built new ones closer to their food supply. Since moving was so much a part of their lives, some Mayans reached places very far indeed from their original homeland.

A Mayan pottery design from Guatemala.

Traveling by canoe, they or others who had learned from them spread out along the coast of the Gulf of Mexico. Many of the adventurers reached the mouth of the Mississippi River. Then, for generation after generation, their descendants kept pushing farther up the great river and the rivers that flowed into it, bringing Mayan corn and culture to the very heart of North America.

The Mayans also traveled overland through Mexico and provided the basis for the famous Aztec civilization that centered around Mexico City. From there Mayan culture spread northward into our Southwest. Mayan corn and the pots in which to store it, Mayan ceremonies to help corn grow, even a little of the Mayan's knowledge of how to build with stone and how to tell from the sun when to plant the fields—all these reached the southwestern part of the United States.

The Southwest was a hungry land where people desperately needed something like corn, and the soil was the kind in which corn seeds would grow. Pueblo culture, which has survived to this day, was the result.

The ruins of Sun Temple stand today on top of Mesa Verde high above the cliff dwellings where its architects and masons made their homes.

Chapter Four

The Ancient Ones

When Indians first moved into the Southwest, perhaps fifteen or twenty thousand years ago, they found a rich, green country—not red-brown and gray as it is now. In those last days of the Ice Age, rain fell in abundance. No droughts baked the land. The lakes and rivers were full. There was plenty of food for mammoths and mastodons—and for men. Game herds of many kinds strayed through lush meadows and forests of hardwood trees, and the first people in the Southwest wandered in pursuit of them. After making their kills they broiled chunks of meat over fires in caves where they slept or near the brush huts that they piled up to give them some protection from the weather.

These wanderers knew nothing of farming. With only stone-pointed spears and throwing sticks as weapons, they fought for existence in that strange, dripping world of long ago.

As time went on, their ways of getting a living had to change, for the whole Southwest was changing. Lakes dried up and rivers shrank as the glaciers retreated toward the Arctic. Leaves withered and fell, and trees died—whole forests of them. Rich grassy meadows disappeared. There was no nourishment for herds of huge animals in the sagebrush and cactus that managed to survive in the new dry climate. Any large beasts that weren't killed by men died off. But men stayed on.

Men could learn and experiment and change their habits. They used the small animals and scrawny plants that clung on in the Southwest mesas as stubbornly as they did, and they borrowed all they could.

As it happened, there was always someone to borrow from. This is one of the most amazing things about the story of the Southwest: it became a sort of melting pot for ideas, for inventions, for people themselves. Many different groups of Indians, from all directions of the compass, crossed this land. Some were seeking new places to live. Others came on trading expeditions. It was this way all over America, too. With only their own feet to carry them, Indians often traveled great distances. Some group was always on the move, and of course it carried all its knowledge along wherever it went. Ideas and techniques spread out over hundreds, even thousands, of miles.

From the Great Plains that lay to the east occasional groups of hunters came to mesa country. Before they turned back in disgust at the poor hunting, they gave the Southwest a kind of house that was much better than the brush shelters. We call it a pit house, and that is what it was. A circular pit was dug about waist deep in the ground and covered with a domelike roof of poles and twigs, thoroughly plastered with mud. Pit houses were a great improvement over brush shelters, for they were warmer in winter and cooler in summer—just as the cellar of a modern house has a more even temperature than the rooms above.

Indians in the Southwest also met Indians from the West Coast, who were skilled gatherers of seeds and roots and who knew how to weave sturdy baskets in which to keep their food.

Storage baskets made life easier for the Southwestern Indian. A woman could put the family food away in containers instead of dumping it loose into a hole in the ground. Baskets also made it possible for people to enjoy new kinds of food. Always before, Indians in the Southwest had eaten their food raw, roasted over a fire, or fried on a hot rock. They had no cooking vessels of any kind. Now the newcomers from the Far West taught women of the mesas to weave baskets fine enough to hold water. By dropping hot rocks into the water, they could boil it and make stews of meat and seeds, roots and leaves.

Indians, probably from the north, brought still another valuable invention to mesa country—the bow and arrow. With this new equipment, which had come over from Asia long after the spear and spear-thrower, a man could be a more efficient hunter. He could carry many more arrows than spears and

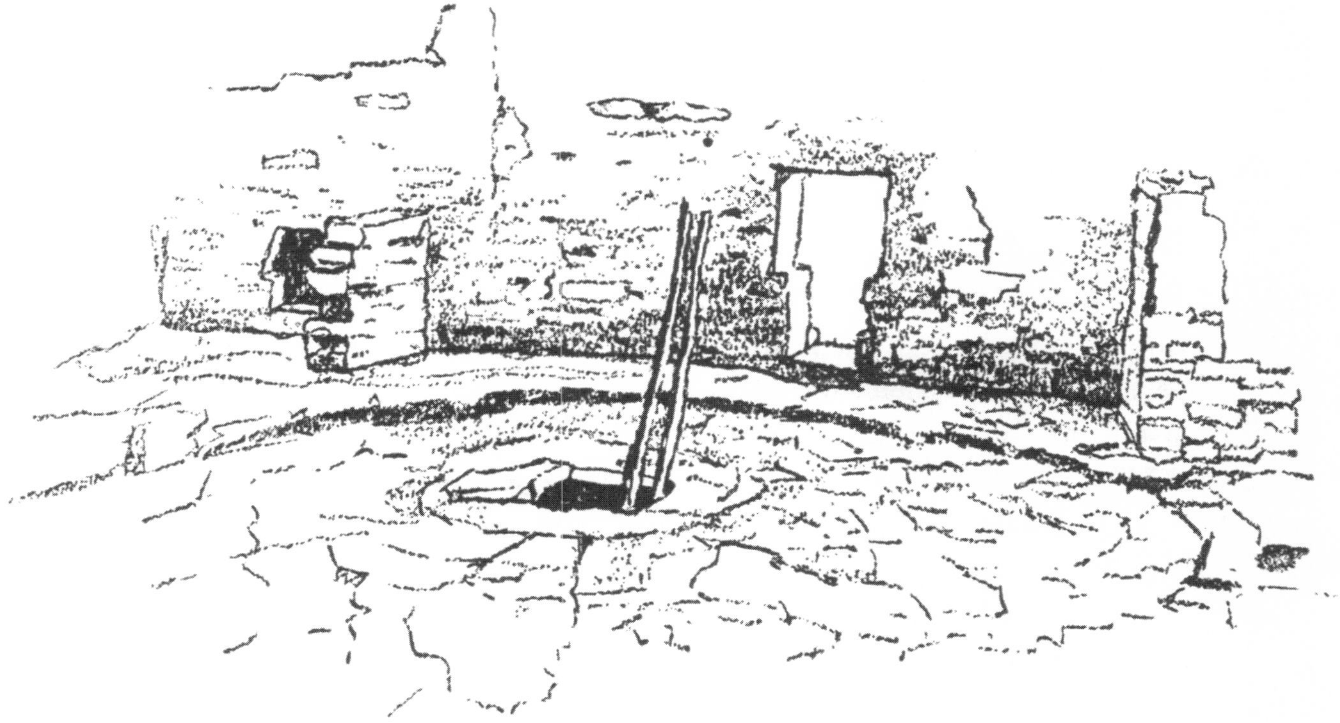

Cliff dwellers entered their underground kivas by a ladder. Notice the T-shaped door in the background of this picture. Mesa Verde doors were low and just broad enough at the top to let a man's shoulders pass through. He rested his hands on the two small ledges and swung his feet over the doorstep through the narrow space at the bottom.

Looking down into a kiva from which the top has been removed. Men sat on the ledge around the room during ceremonies. The small circle in the foreground is a hole called the si-pa-pu or spirit hole. Through it men communicated with the gods who lived in the underworld. The larger circle is the fire pit. Behind it stands an upright slab of stone to deflect the draft of air that came down the ventilator shaft through the square hole behind it.

he could make a dozen shots in the time it used to take him to throw and recover his spear just once.

The innovations that came from the east, north, and west were important. But the most important of all came from Mexico. Traders and possibly wandering Indians who moved into mesa country from the south brought with them the seeds of squash, beans, and corn.

Up to now a seed had been something just to pick and eat. But each one of the new seeds was worth ten or fifty or a hundred times as much as a wild one. A kernel of corn that took root in the ground produced a stalk with several ears, and each ear had scores of kernels. A field of corn could feed a whole family during cold winter months.

Very soon the inhabitants of the Southwest stopped roaming. They stayed close to the fields where their wonderful new food grew. Neighbors gathered together in larger groups than before and shared the work in the fields. After a while, they moved out of their pit houses and built solid ones of stone or adobe clay. Women learned to make clay cooking pots in a few hours instead of spending days weaving baskets.

Scores of towns, or pueblos, as the Spanish called them, grew up, no two exactly alike. In some the people spoke the language of Indians from the east. In others, the language was that of northerners. Eventually, Pueblo Indians spoke four distinct languages—and they still do. Some built houses of stone; others used sun-dried bricks of adobe mud.

In spite of their differences, the pattern of life in all the Pueblo villages was very much the same. They all raised corn and they held special ceremonies that they thought would bring precious summer rains and help the plants grow. In fact, corn and ceremonies were inseparable, for the people who brought corn from the far off land of the Mayas brought the corn gods and rain gods, too.

Now a very interesting thing happened. The new gods and ceremonies blended easily with the simpler religion that the hunting people had had when they still lived in brush shelters or pit houses. In the old days, each family conducted its own ceremonies in its own home. When they began living together in pueblos, they held ceremonies in larger and larger groups—but they held them in rooms that resembled the old pit houses, for even while they learned new things, they clung tenaciously to the past. The round, sunken rooms became the community centers that we call kivas. As generation followed

The ruins of the largest village at Mesa Verde, Colorado, are called Cliff Palace, but it was not really the home of kings or princes. Farmers occupied its more than two hundred rooms which were perched high above a canyon floor and were sheltered by a huge overhanging slab of sandstone. In addition, twenty-three kivas served as ceremonial rooms and meeting places for the village.

generation, men dug the kivas deeper into the earth. Finally, they were completely underground.

The new religion flourished and spread in every direction. There were kivas in villages out on the dry plains, along the river bottoms, in great shallow caves high up in cliffs.

Some of the Pueblo people had built their towns in the cliffs for protection from enemy raiders. For two hundred years or so, these cliff dwellers perched in their natural fortresses high above the canyon floors. Farmers went to and from the fields by ladders or ropes or footholds cut in the soft sandstone. Women carried water up to their homes in pots balanced on their heads.

Everywhere in Pueblo land life grew richer and more beautiful. Corn gave the villages a plentiful food supply, so the Indians had time to spend making all kinds of decorations and small conveniences and comforts. Men made tools for straightening crooked, scrubby wood to make good arrows. For music at their ceremonies they made drums, rattles, and flutes. From the drill with which they kindled fires they evolved a drill for boring holes in turquoise or in shells to form beads.

Dance rattles made of turtle shell, gourd, bark, and skin.

Cottonseeds came from the south, too, and the cliff dwellers learned how to weave it into cloth and twist it into cords. This not only made for more comfort and beauty, but it also meant that the women could let their hair grow long. In the old days, they had cut it off with sharp-edged shells or stone knives to weave into belts, straps, or cords.

The urge to experiment and change and decorate was everywhere. For a while, women molded the shape of children's heads. Possibly the idea came from Central America, along with so many other things, but cliff dwellers had their own variation on the Mayan style of deformation. Instead of sloping the forehead to a peak, mothers tied their babies' heads snugly against cradle boards and flattened them at the back.

We know so much about the Indians who lived in cliff dwellings because their homes are still standing—sometimes with all their household goods in place. The dry Southwestern climate has preserved many cliff villages almost exactly the way they were about seven hundred years ago, although the people themselves moved away. Some joined other pueblos. Some built new towns in other parts of the Southwest. A few must have left quite suddenly, for archeologists have found pots still sitting on the ashes of cooking fires.

There may have been many reasons why the cliff dwellers abandoned their homes. Since the knowledge of writing had not reached them from Mexico, they left no record to explain their departure. We do know, however, from studying tree rings in the beams of the Mesa Verde ruins that a great drought began in the year 1276 and lasted to 1299. Crops failed and the people in the cliffs went hungry. No doubt the fierce raiding Navahos and Apaches who invaded Pueblo land about this time were hungry, too. Their attacks in search of food must have grown more frequent and more terrible. Probably the cliff dwellers thought they had offended the gods of the rain, and they decided to go to another place where the gods would not be so angry with them.

Like the ancient cliff dwellers, the near-by Pueblo and Navaho Indians today use cradle boards for their babies.

At any rate, they did leave. So did neighboring people whose homes were not in the cliffs. The inhabitants of a very large village that we call Pueblo Bonito fled from Chaco Canyon, New Mexico, perhaps a hundred years before the cliff dwellings were abandoned. These people had built their pueblo in the form of one big apartment house. (Not until 1892 in New York City was a larger one built.) There were eight hundred rooms in Pueblo Bonito, constructed around an open plaza in the shape of a great capital "D." On the curving side the houses rose to a height of four stories, and one-story rooms lined the straight side, so that a continuous wall of buildings surrounded the plaza. The only way to get in was by climbing a ladder. Obviously these Indians had enemies whom they had constantly to guard against.

We don't know why they left Pueblo Bonito, but we do know a great deal about how they lived because the huge apartment house is still standing and archeologists have studied it thoroughly. The town was rich in lovely white pottery covered with interesting angular designs painted black. Like the cliff dwellers, the people of Pueblo Bonito had warm robes woven from feathers of the turkeys they had tamed and kept in large flocks. They wove cotton blankets, too, on large looms, working with yarns they dyed in various colors from

Pueblo Bonito, the largest of the ancient apartment-house villages of the Southwest, was built like a fortress at the foot of a cliff in a canyon bottom.

roots and plants. Sandals were fashioned from the tough leaves and fibers of the yucca plant. Mats made of reeds or rushes covered the floors and hung across doorways.

The inhabitants of Pueblo Bonito were famous jewelers. They carved little stone pendants in the form of animals and birds. They made beads out of sea-shells carried all the way from the coast of California. Their greatest achievement was in work with turquoise. They fitted tiny bits of this sky-blue stone into mosaics and strung highly polished beads of it into necklaces. Excavators dug up one necklace that had twenty-five hundred beads, each one carefully shaped and drilled.

From the leaves of the yucca plant come long, tough fibers which Pueblo Indians used for making sandals, paint brushes, and sometimes even combination brooms and hairbrushes. From the yucca fruit they made food and from the roots a lathery shampoo.

Some of the skill that went into making jewelry also went into the masonry of Pueblo Bonito. The sandstone in the great walls was shaped and fitted with great precision. Small stones and large ones joined perfectly together, and in parts of the wall the builders even went to the trouble of laying the masonry in bands to form a pleasant pattern.

Here, as in every pueblo that was more than one story high, the ceiling of one room was the floor of the room above. First, the builders at Pueblo Bonito rested pine beams, from which they had peeled the bark, on top of the stone walls. Then they placed light poles at right angles to the beams. Next came heavy mats woven from peeled willow branches. On top of these they placed finer mats made of splints of juniper wood. They then piled on a thick layer of the clayey soil and packed it down until it was as hard as cement.

Pueblo Bonito was only one of many villages in Chaco Canyon built in this general way. Life in all of them was much like life in the cliff dwellings of Mesa Verde and

Besides all the other uses they made of the yucca plant, Pueblo Indians also made a lathery shampoo from its roots.

in scores of other communities that have been abandoned for seven hundred years or more.

A visitor at Pueblo Bonito today can scarcely imagine that the twelve hundred people who lived there at any one time could grow corn or even get water to drink. During much of the year the Chaco River is dry, and the country around is a deeply eroded wasteland. But one thousand years ago a

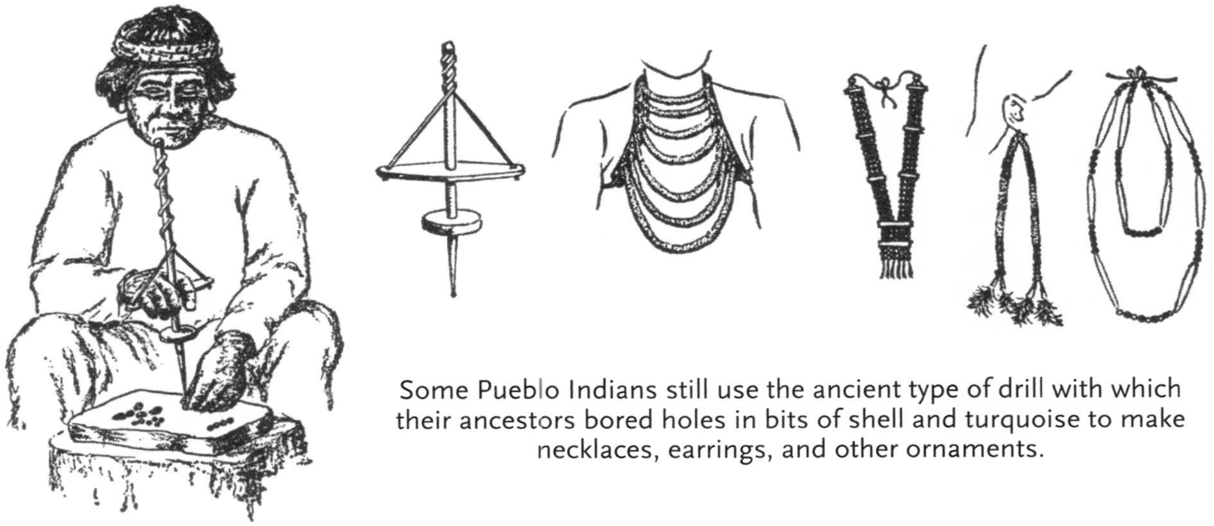

Some Pueblo Indians still use the ancient type of drill with which their ancestors bored holes in bits of shell and turquoise to make necklaces, earrings, and other ornaments.

pine forest must have covered the top of the mesa that looms over the village. There is no other way to explain the big beams in the houses. The land must have been covered with grass that protected it from erosion, and certainly there was enough water in the river to serve the needs of the people and to nourish the willows they used in making their floors. But all this changed, and possibly the people who lived there were partly to blame. By cutting down the trees and by farming large areas of land, they may have started the ruinous erosion. Forest fires and drought may have destroyed the woodlands.

Also, this largest pueblo was under heavy attack from warlike raiders. Excavators have found evidences of headlong flight in the great courtyard and in the houses. But the Pueblo people as such did not disappear. They continued to live in villages along the Rio Grande and its tributaries and in a few isolated spots in the desert where spring water seeped out of layers of sandstone that absorbed moisture from higher, damper ground many miles away. There the early Spanish explorers found them, and there we can visit them today.

Hopi Indians still live in Walpi, a village their ancestors built on a high bluff centuries ago.

Chapter Five

Towns in the Desert

THE OLDEST INHABITED towns in the United States stand on the high, sunny mesas of the Southwest. Most ancient of all is Oraibi in Arizona. Indians have lived and farmed there for the last eight hundred years. At Acoma, New Mexico, people have lived in well-built stone apartment houses on the top of a towering rock for almost that long. And there are nearly thirty more pueblos, some of which have stood on their present sites for centuries.

What is the secret of their persistence? Why have many Pueblo ways continued to such a large extent unchanged since the days of the cliff dwellings and Chaco Canyon? There is no quick, easy answer, but we may begin to understand if we take a closer look at a typical village in the days before the arrival of the Spanish conquistadors.

The pueblo was a busy place. On autumn days, barefoot women in sleeveless cotton dresses worked at preparing and storing food for the wintertime. The top of each square family room was gay with many-colored ears of corn drying in the sun. Yellow and red and purple and speckled ears made splashes of brightness against the gray-brown building walls. Men, wearing cloth or buckskin breechcloths and sandals of plaited yucca leaves, carried on their backs great loads of almost smokeless juniper wood from distant hills. Gray pots simmered outdoors on dozens of little fires. Small naked boys chased turkeys and played with dogs. From inside a few of the homes came the shrill cries of gaudy macaws which had been brought from far off Mexico.

In a wicker cage on top of one house, an angry-looking old eagle glowered down. He lived a life of captivity, not because he was a lovable pet, but because his feathers were highly prized for use in ceremonies. Here and there old men squatted in the sunlight, telling stories to their sisters' sons or grandsons whom they were supposed to instruct. In a few days all the young men would be through with the last of their farm work and many of them would go off hunting for deer.

A girl and one young man, who was resting after a trip for wood, took turns brushing each other's long straight black hair with a bundle of dried grama grass. One end of the bundle was cut squarely across to make a stiff brush; the other served as a broom for keeping the floor of the girl's house neat. This hair-brushing ceremony told the whole pueblo that the two young people had decided to be married.

Off in the distance a shaggy uncombed stranger hid behind a clump of rabbit bush and studied the village. He was a member of the wandering tribe that called itself Dineh—the People—the tribe we know as Navaho. He had no idea about Pueblo ceremonies, but he did know that the crops were gathered and that the dark storage rooms underneath the second story of the pueblo would be full of corn, beans, and dried squash. Warm blankets made from turkey feathers or woven strips of rabbit fur hung from pegs in every room, and cotton blankets, too.

The stranger's own people had no such store of food to keep them through the hungry winter months, no luxurious blankets, and none of the beautiful jewelry and ornaments that the Pueblos wore. They were nomads who lived by hunting and by gathering the roots and seeds of wild plants. For a long time they had been looking for a place that offered them enough to eat, and here it seemed that they had found it. A quick raid on the village would provide food for weeks.

In ancient times people called the Hohokam built enormous irrigation ditches to water their fields south of the main Pueblo area. They made pots like this one.

However, the attack might not be as easy as it looked. A pueblo was like a turtle. At the least sign of danger it could draw into its shell. The rooms were more or less stacked together, apartment house fashion, and none of them had doors. To get inside, you had to climb first to the roof, then down ladders through holes in the ceilings of the rooms. In time of danger, the Pueblos simply pulled up the ladders that led from the ground to the first story.

The stranger saw that a raid on the village would have to be well planned. He and the other warriors in his band must bring something to use for climbing. Since they didn't know how to make ladders, they decided dead tree trunks would do.

Day after day the stranger watched and waited, until he saw most of the Pueblo men leave for a hunt. That night the raiders moved stealthily toward the village, as silent as mountain lions stalking deer. But from a rooftop, a Pueblo watchman spied them and gave the alarm. Boys and old men rushed to the roofs with war clubs, stone knives, and bows and arrows ready. Mothers snatched up the cradle boards on which their babies were tied and climbed ladders to the protection of the highest rooms. A few of the raiders managed to scramble up the tree trunks they had brought such a distance. In the dark there rose terrible shouts and the confused noise of hand-to-hand struggle. But the defenders knew every inch of their pueblo, and soon the strangers, bloody and defeated, ran off into the safety of the night.

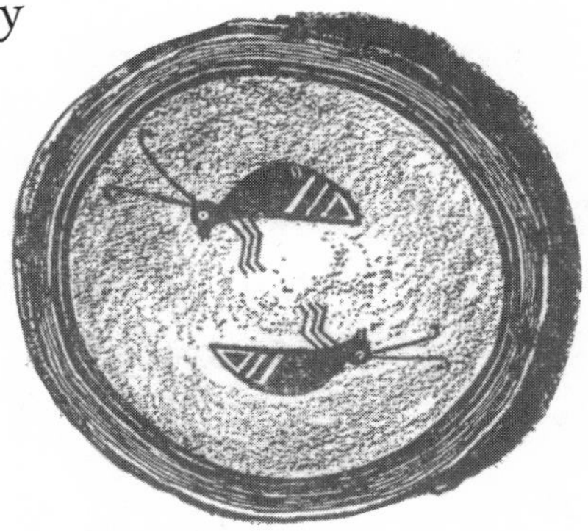

An ancient people, the Mogollons, drew human figures, animals, and even insects on their pottery. This design is from a bowl.

This raid had failed, but others succeeded. The peaceful Pueblos often lost many of their possessions. Occasionally the enemy carried off women and children, but mainly they wanted corn. The Pueblos had a never-ending struggle to protect it. They had a never-ending struggle to grow it, too.

Pueblo men and boys began their farm work early each year—very early, indeed. Often in the cold winter weather of February they were out in their fields, beginning to protect the soil against heavy rains that would come in spring and again in late summer. Across every little depression or gully they built dams of earth and brush to prevent erosion. They made fences of brush to check the winds that blew away soil and lashed too roughly at the tender corn shoots.

Later on, everybody in the pueblo waited eagerly for word from an important man called the Sun Watcher, who was the keeper of the village calendar. Like the Mayan priests, he told people when to plant their crops, but he had to make his calculations without the help of arithmetic or written records. The traders and farmers who had brought corn and corn-growing ceremonies to the Pueblos had not been able to pass along the knowledge of reading and writing for the very good reason that they did not have it themselves. So the Sun Watcher had to tell the seasons, or "steps of the year," by keeping track of the places where the sun rose in relation to local landmarks. When it came up from behind a certain hill, he knew that the danger of frost had passed. On that day, early in May, he shouted the news to the village.

Men and boys set out for the fields, carrying special sticks for digging and fawn-skin bags full of precious seed. They had prayed over the bags and had sprinkled them with holy cornmeal and sacred pollens. They prayed in the cornfields, too, before they started work. Often, in the center of a field, a man set up a prayer stick decorated with the feathers of birds that were supposed to bring rain.

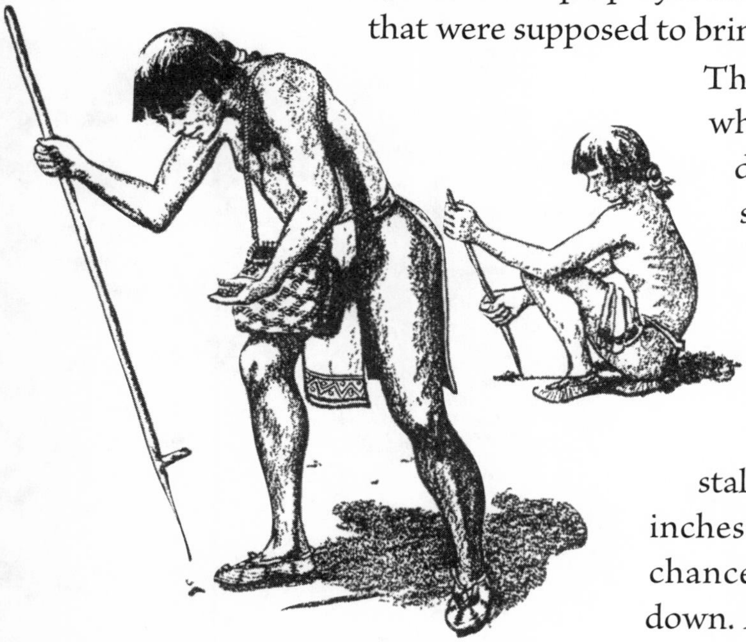

Pueblo Indians, using sharp-pointed digging sticks, made deep holes in which to plant their corn.

The stick was like the hub of a wagon wheel. Radiating out from it in every direction were rows of withered stalks—last year's corn plants. They had been left as markers, so that seed would not be planted in the same spot two years running. Now, with the digging sticks, the men made holes between the old stalks, sometimes a foot or even eighteen inches deep. In the dry season there was a chance that moisture would stay that far down. Also, the holes could not be too close together, for during the hot summer days there would not be enough moisture in the

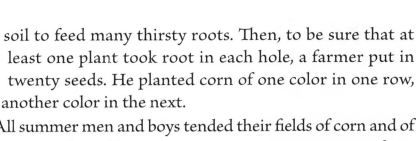

Indians of the Hopi pueblos believed in gods called kachinas, and they carved dolls out of cottonwood root to represent the gods. Dancers at ceremonies often wore kachina masks that looked exactly like the dolls.

soil to feed many thirsty roots. Then, to be sure that at least one plant took root in each hole, a farmer put in twenty seeds. He planted corn of one color in one row, another color in the next.

All summer men and boys tended their fields of corn and of cotton, squash, and beans. Women sometimes came out from the village for picnic parties, and day after day the children had fun in the brilliant sunlight chasing crows away.

The fields often lay far from the pueblo, and the fastest way to get there was to run. When the men and boys were not trotting to work or back, they often had running games. One of these was kick-the-stick. Teams of barefoot racers might run as far as twenty, thirty, or even forty miles, kicking sticks along the ground the whole way. Some of the Pueblos believed that this kind of race would help to bring rains, for the tumbling of the stick along the ground was like the motion of dead wood being carried down a swift stream.

While the men and boys were at work in the fields, women and girls kept busy at home. Every day they spent three or four hours grinding corn for bread, cakes, soups, and other dishes that were the main part of every meal. They mixed ground corn with dried mushrooms or with the powdered roots of plants, and rolled it into dumplings that they steamed in pots. Sometimes they sweetened the corn with the dried fruit of the yucca plant. They baked corn bread of various kinds. They spiced their food with the many seasonings they made from dried leaves or flowers, or from flower pollen. Pueblo women turned the most unlikely plants to some use. Even milkweed juice made chewing gum.

Most of these good things had to be stored and later cooked in clay pots. Pottery making was a woman's job, too. For cooking, she made plain gray

Pueblo women and girls often sang in unison as they ground corn meal by rubbing the grain between a small stone called a mano and a larger stone called a metate.

A modern Zuni pueblo pot. This is used as a drum with a piece of skin stretched across its top.

vessels because they got sooty in the fire, but those she used for storage cupboards or at ceremonies could be as beautiful as she wished.

Each village had its own particular style of pottery that was like a trademark. A Pueblo could tell where any article had been made by its color, pattern, and design. A beautifully polished bowl with black zigzag designs on a pearly white background came from Mesa Verde. It had been fired in such a way that air was kept from circulating around it. Dishes from the Kayenta area had red, black, and white designs painted on a background of orange or yellow made by letting in air as the pottery was fired.

A woman took pride in her pots and in the gay appearance they gave to the strong, square room that was her home. It was literally *her* home, for she owned it. Either she inherited it from her mother's family or the family built it specially for her, and there she had authority. All the food and household goods were hers. When she married she never went to live with her husband, whose real home was with his mother. The groom always came to the bride's house as a sort of permanent guest.

An ancient Pueblo pitcher.

Proud though she was of her home, no woman could boast that it was larger than any other. There were neither very rich nor very poor among the Pueblos. They lived a life of share-and-share-alike. Although each family had special fields to farm, it would have seemed silly to the Pueblos to talk of individuals owning land. The land was there for the whole tribe to use.

Just as women had special privileges in their homes, men had privileges in the underground kivas, which were a combination of clubhouse and church. Here the men gathered, especially during the long winter months when there was little farm work to do. They wove blankets, told stories, gave instruction to the younger boys, and held ceremonies that sometimes lasted for many days.

Everything in Pueblo life was closely tied to religion in one way or another. Although they had learned how to use the plants and animals and stones and the dry earth about them, there were many things in nature that they did not yet understand. Droughts came and crops failed. People died of disease. Enemies appeared and did great damage. The world was not a simple place. The Pueblos, like people everywhere, used energy and imagination in an effort to get along in harmony with the mysterious forces that worked on their lives.

Since no real cause could be seen for disease or drought or bad luck in general, spirits or gods must be the explanation, they thought. The spirits or gods were responsible for all the good things, too. And so, as a way of pleasing them or showing gratitude, the Pueblos held religious ceremonies with dancing and costumes and singing. Many of the ceremonies were as beautiful and exciting to watch as plays. Indeed, the Pueblos enjoyed them as much as we enjoy watching television or going to the theater. More important, every dance or song was a prayer. Each ceremony had a story behind it, a story about the gods who brought rain or made the precious corn grow, or did something else important in the Pueblos' lives. Each god had his particular costume and ritual, as in the Eagle Dance where the participants were covered with down from head to toe and had eagle feathers fluttering along their arms. With arms outstretched they imitated the soaring of that majestic bird of the mountains whose fierceness and courage they so respected.

Different religious societies had charge of different ceremonies. A man often belonged to more than one of these groups, and he was also a member of the clan into which he was born. (A clan consisted of all the people who were descended from one female ancestor.) Some of the religious societies were limited to members of one clan, but others had members from various clans.

Since a Pueblo was such a complicated place, full of organizations each with its own special importance, the lives of all the people interlocked in many ways. Their apartment house life and their communal farming showed that they felt a need for being close together. As a result, there was always considerable pressure on individuals to do everything exactly as the whole group

A Zuni pueblo woman weaving. In other pueblos weaving was the men's work.

thought it should be done. As time passed, the right way came to be almost always the traditional way.

As droughts and enemies drove the Pueblos into a smaller area, these peaceful farmers became increasingly defensive and conservative. This people who had begun by eagerly absorbing new ideas and making all sorts of innovations had almost ceased to experiment by the time the Spanish settled in their country about the year 1600. Then came a struggle between the old Pueblo customs and the new ones from Europe. Because the barren Southwest did not attract Europeans in great numbers, the Pueblos were allowed to stay on in their ancient homeland. But, although the Pueblos' insistence on keeping their old beliefs and customs held them together and helped them survive as a group, the great spurt of life generated by the Mayans had run its full course.

Kachina dancers wearing masks to represent different gods.

Chapter Six

The Mound Builders

When Père Marquette sailed down the Mississippi River in 1673 he was astounded to look up one day and see a pair of weird figures—part bear, part fish, and part deer—carved high on a bluff near what is now Alton, Illinois. Unfortunately he was not interested in investigating these rock carvings, but later explorers found only a short distance away an enormous pyramidal mound of earth, the Cahokia mound, in Illinois.

This mound is standing today, along with many thousands of other mounds—in the form of pyramids, cones, and beasts and birds—all over the eastern part of the United States and for some distance west of the Mississippi. These heaps of earth have been abandoned for so long that neighboring Indian tribes remember nothing of their history.

All sorts of people from archeologists to curious boys have dug into the mounds. Many of them yield nothing but bones. Others have been virtual treasure houses of things made by a vanished people. The largest were simply earthworks with nothing inside them, but there is no doubt that man once built them.

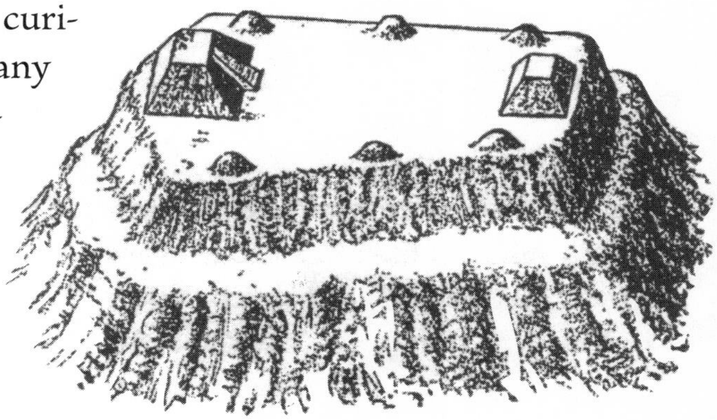

These mounds are a far cry from the abandoned pueblos in the arid Southwest, where the dry atmosphere has preserved organic matter, including human bodies. The mounds were built along rivers or in low, damp places where almost everything made of wood or skin rotted and disappeared. Only things that did not decay in this climate have survived—tools and ornaments of stone, copper, shell, and bone.

Who were the people who constructed these mounds? Actually no one knows. The mystery of the Mound Builders has intrigued people curious about the first Americans ever since the days of Thomas Jefferson, who was one of the first to delve into the earth heaps. But by piecing together clues gleaned from the digging up of hundreds of mounds we have a fairly good idea of who the Mound Builders were and why they vanished so completely.

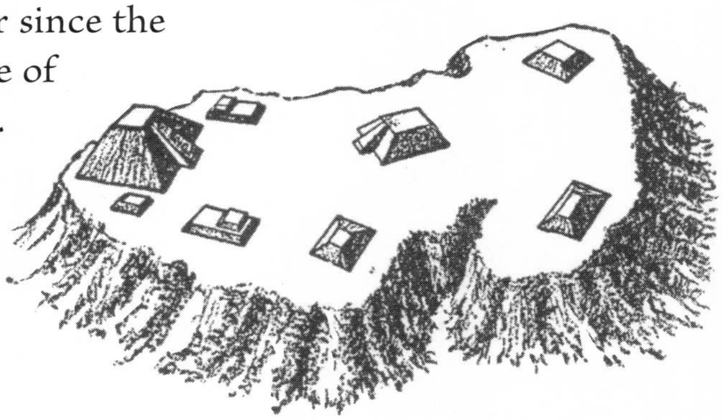

Over a thousand years ago, about the time when groups of Indians from Central America were migrating to the Southwest, some Mayans were traveling northward along the coast of the Gulf of Mexico. When they reached the mouth of the Mississippi River, they discovered the entrance to a vast new world where the soil and the climate were perfect for growing corn. People were already living along the Mississippi and its many tributaries, but they were not farmers. They were hunters who still used the spear and spear-thrower, for they had not learned about bows and arrows.

Archeologists aren't quite sure what happened when the Mayans and their corn met the Mississippi Valley hunters and their spears. Some say the

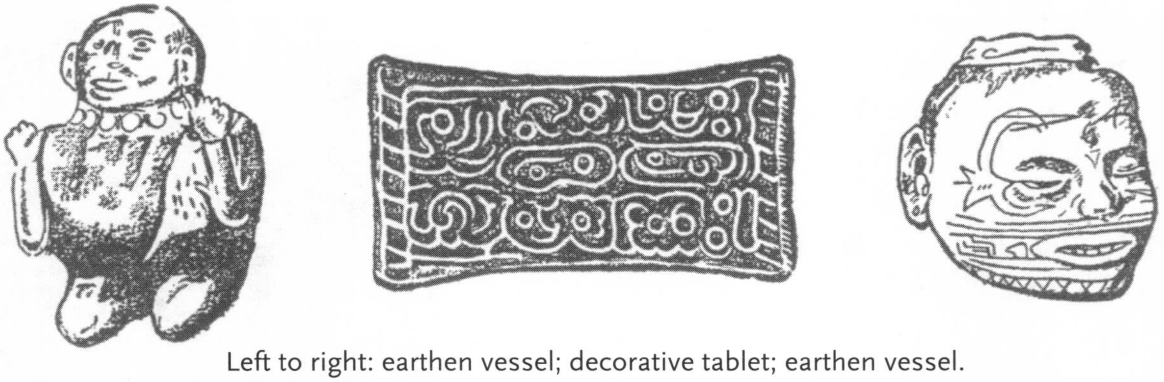

Left to right: earthen vessel; decorative tablet; earthen vessel.

Mayans came in great numbers and, after conquering the more primitive tribes, settled down to live in the wilderness very much as they had lived back home. Other people believe that only a few Mayans reached the Mississippi and that their knowledge of farming and handicrafts spread gradually among the hunting people.

Regardless of how the change began, there is no doubt that the corn the Mayans brought started a great spurt of life in the heart of North America. All along the river banks people sowed fields of grain which guaranteed them a bigger and steadier supply of food than they could get from fish in the streams and game in the woods. Hunters changed into farmers—or at least their wives did. Villages grew up near the corn patches. People worked together in the fields and took part in ceremonies together. They developed some loose kind of village government.

Along with their corn, the Mayans brought their pottery and the techniques of making it. They brought their love of jewelry and the many skills

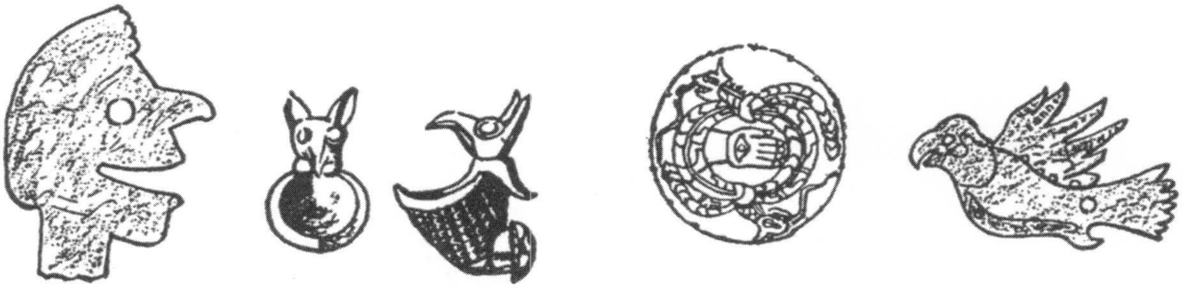

Left to right: head carved out of mica; two views of an earthenware pipe bowl; plate with knotted serpent design; flying eagle modeled in copper.

required to cut and polish small bits of stone, to bore tiny holes, or to pound lumps of pure copper into delicate shapes. As corn spread north to Canada and east to the Atlantic, certain Mayan arts and crafts followed close behind. So did parts of Mayan ceremonies and legends.

Eventually the new farmers in North America began to worship the sun, just as Central American people had done. They held similar ceremonies to please the spirits that made the corn grow, and they practiced the gruesome ritual of terror and hope involving human sacrifice. Since farming and sacrifice both had come from the south, various Mississippi Valley tribes thought the two belonged together.

Neck ornament carved on shell.

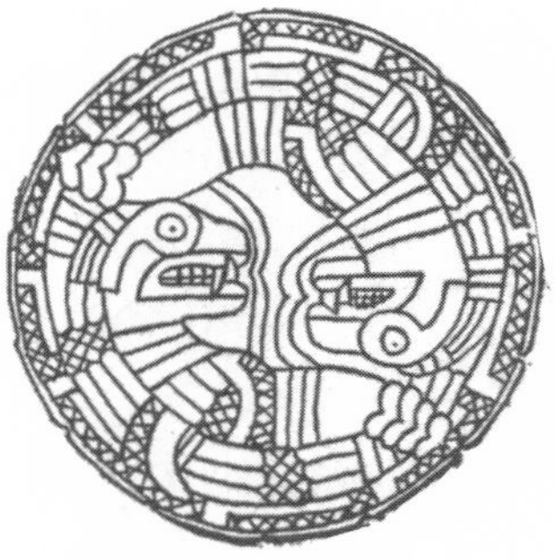

Plate with feathered serpent design.

Quite likely the Mayan pioneers came from the common people rather than from the priesthood or the nobility, for crafts and skills flourished in the new country but not the writing, reading, arithmetic, and knowledge of architecture which the priests and nobles alone possessed. It was the common people who had done the actual work of heaping earth into great pyramids in order to raise temples toward the sun and stars. This the Mayan immigrants to the Mississippi region remembered well, and they undoubtedly told their children and grandchildren about the mounds in their homeland. As time went on, the tales about earth pyramids grew more and more vague and mixed up. But if making artificial hills was a way to please the spirits, the tribes who had learned farming from the Mayans were willing to try it. So they built mounds.

At first the mounds were built to honor the dead, who were an important part of the Indians' spirit world. A religious revival swept the country in the wake of the spread of corn. In some places people buried gifts and supplies for the spirits of the dead to use on their journey to the Happy Hunting Grounds. Occasionally a practical tribe used its earthworks as a fortification, for many Mound Builders were having the same kind of trouble with wandering raiders that the Pueblo farmers of the Southwest had. In other places, particularly in Wisconsin and Ohio, they built strange effigy mounds in the shapes of quails, turtles, bears, deer, or snakes, which were probably the sacred totems of the tribes that so laboriously shaped them. Today the great Brush Creek Serpent Mound in Ohio and the Elephant Mound in Wisconsin are only two of the many effigy mounds that are still standing.

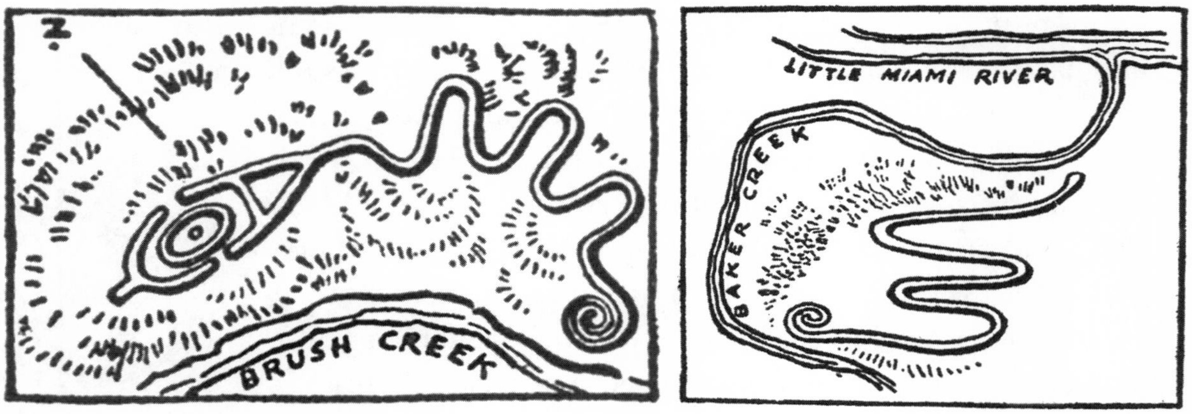

Indians of the Mississippi valley built mounds in many shapes. Some were flat-topped pyramids; others were cones; still others were shaped like birds or snakes.

In one form or another, mounds appeared over a huge area, but for a long time the Mound Builders never thought of setting temples on the vast earthen foundations. This part of the Mayan pyramid idea had been lost. Then, apparently, about the year 1300 new immigrants came from Central America, bringing with them the true Mayan practice of building flat-topped pyramids as a base for their temples. Temple mounds spread all over the South and up the Mississippi. There are more than three hundred in what is now the city of East St. Louis. One of these is the Cahokia mound which is one hundred feet high and covers an area greater than that of the largest of the great pyramids of Egypt.

Men and women and perhaps children heaped up all that earth by hand. First, they loosened the soil with simple digging sticks or with hoes made of large shells. Shoulder blades of deer or buffalo were the trowels and shovels with which they scooped the earth into carrying bags made of skin or into baskets woven from strips of bark.

Year after year the mounds grew. Although the work must have been slow and tedious, Mound Builder life itself was full of variety and color. In every direction people carried on trade that was unbelievably vast. From the Rocky Mountains came grizzly bear teeth for necklaces and black volcanic glass to be made into knives and arrow points. The Allegheny Mountains to the east produced sheets of mica for mirrors and ornaments. Soft, easily carved soapstone came from Delaware, and seashells of different shapes and sizes from the Gulf of Mexico. Chunks of pure copper mined by Mound Builders in the Great Lakes region traveled far to the south, and gold from Mexico worked its way north.

Craftsmen put all of these things to good use. Some of them carved beautiful stone tobacco pipes in the form of realistic animals and birds. Others specialized in jewelry. They drilled fine holes in the pearls that came from shellfish in the rivers and set them along with precious stones in bear teeth. They pounded copper into earrings, bracelets, headdresses, and breastplates that were worn for decoration. Other metalworkers beat copper into chisels, axes, knives, needles, fishhooks, and even buttons. In one Ohio Mound Builder tribe—the Hopewell people—the chief wore a special headdress made of wood or leather topped with deer antlers. Around his neck hung a string

Pipe bowl in the shape of a dog.

Snake carved from mica.

of silver beads to which a human jaw was attached like a locket. His sleeveless deerskin jacket was sewn with hundreds of pearls. A fashionable warrior of the tribe had two topknots of hair, one at the front and one at the back of his head. All the rest of his hair was shaved off with a sharp stone or more likely pulled out with tweezers made of mussel shells. His face and the bare patches on his head were painted white; his body from the waist up was painted a kind of purplish red. Except possibly for moccasins, his only garment was a small breechcloth decorated with pearls or beads made of shells or bear teeth. In his ears he wore enormous copper earrings and around his neck a pearl or tooth necklace.

Women of the tribe had wraparound skirts made of red cloth. They wore ankle-high moccasins made of animal skin, and both their skirts and their moccasins were decorated with pearls. Like men they wore big copper ear ornaments, but their hair, except for ceremonial occasions, was dressed much more simply—just parted in the middle and made into a single braid at the back.

How do we know all these things about the long-vanished Hopewell people? They left small carved and painted figures of themselves. More important, they were Burial Mound Builders who made special graves for chiefs and priests and their wives. Usually they filled the graves with lavish gifts—tools

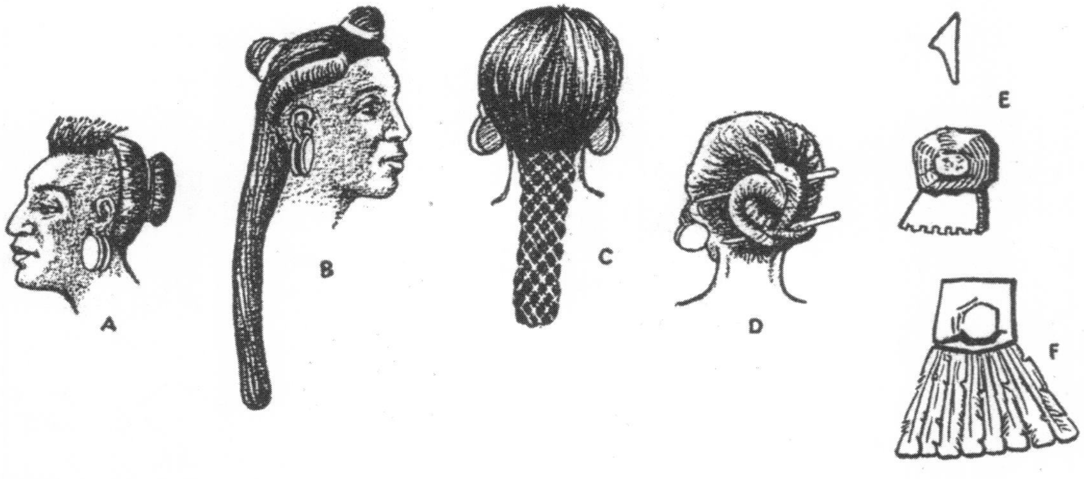

A. Hopewell man's hair dress—note the large ear ornament. B. Hopewell woman's ceremonial hairdress. C. and D. Hopewell woman's ordinary hair dress. E. and F. Bustles worn by ceremonial dancers. (From Archeology of the Eastern United States, edited by James B. Griffin, University of Chicago Press, 1952.)

A. Hopewell man wearing a breastplate and necklace of shell and pearls with a pendant made of a wolf's jaw. In his hand is a copper chopping tool. B. Hopewell official in ceremonial costume covered with pearl beads. The necklace is made of silver beads with a human jaw as a pendant. C. Hopewell mother and child. D. Hopewell woman ceremonial dancer. (From Archeology of the Eastern United States, edited by James B. Griffin, University of Chicago Press, 1952.)

and weapons and luxuries for the deceased to use or enjoy on the journey to the future life. These gifts to the dead, which archeologists have found in mound after mound, reveal how people lived and worked, what decorations they fancied, the kind of pipe they liked to smoke. By a curious piece of luck we can even tell what kind of clothes they wore. In some of the graves, fabrics were buried close to ornaments and tools of copper, and the copper made it possible for the fibers of cotton or bark to escape the normal process of decay.

Graves have yielded treasures of all kinds—some quite as tempting to ancient marauders as to modern professors. One man had 60,000 freshwater pearls buried with his bones! Such wealth was bound to bring trouble from the more primitive hunting tribes, and the Mound Builders were constantly at war.

This warfare was an endless drain on the Mound Builders' strength, but something else probably weakened them even more. About five hundred years ago, a kind of religious frenzy swept over the country. The Mound Builders had always paid a great deal of attention to death and burial, which developed into a special cult of death. The people seemed almost afraid to live, and their priests taught them to worship death itself.

This fanatical cult of death spread from village to village at just about the time the white conquerors began to arrive from Europe. Then suddenly the strange custom of building mounds stopped. The first Spanish expedition to cross the southern part of the country saw the last mounds being built.

Mound building lasted in all about a thousand years, and no one can be sure why it ended, any more than we can be sure we know all the reasons for the disappearance of the Mayan civilization. But in both civilizations an enormous amount of energy went into building great religious works. In both, religion revolved more and more around death. The priests offered no help at all to their people who had real problems to face in the day-to-day work of farming and defending their homes from outside attack.

When mound building stopped, a civilization died with it. The Mound Builders' crafts were either forgotten or survived imperfectly. Pottery was never so beautiful again in North America. The art of beating copper into tools and jewelry disappeared. Nobody remembered how to make mirrors and decorations cut from mica. Perhaps primitive raiders actually killed off the skilled craftsmen among the Mound Builders.

But farmers remained, and so did corn, beans, and squash, and gradually more and more of the raiders settled down with the descendants of the Mound Builders. They lived and planted their fields close to the one hundred thousand heaps of earth that were all that apparently remained of a rich culture. In many of these tribes, however, beliefs and ceremonies persisted that came down from the Mayans by way of the Mound Builders.

Chapter Seven

Warpath and Peace Pipe

THE IROQUOIS WERE not one tribe of Indians but first five and later six tribes who lived largely in the woodlands of what is now the State of New York. Their domain stretched from the Cherokee lands in Tennessee north to Hudson's Bay, and westward from southern New England to the Mississippi River. They got their name of "Iroquois" from the French in Canada, but they had another name for themselves—Hodenosaunee, or People of the Longhouse, for like the cliff dwellings of the Pueblos, the longhouse was the home of the Iroquois and the symbol of their strength.

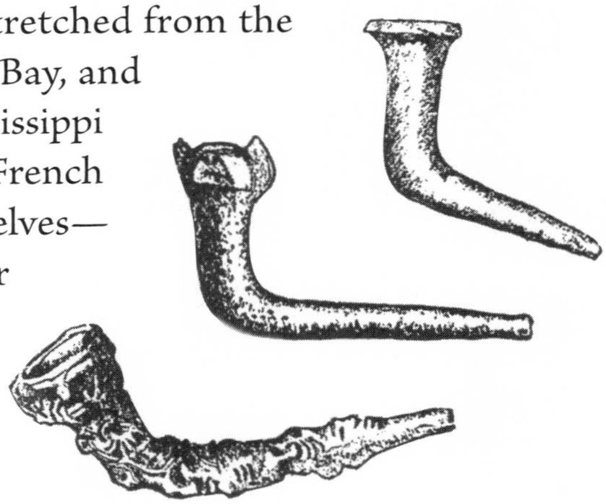

The Iroquois made elbow-shaped pipes of clay and inserted a reed tube as a mouthpiece.

More contradictory stories have been told about the Iroquois tribes than about any other Indians. Early white settlers who met these stern warriors of the woodlands thought them the most cruel and terrifying people in the world. But white boys and girls who were kidnapped from frontier settlements and adopted by an Iroquois tribe often refused to return home. Their captors turned out to be kindly and lovable friends, for the Iroquois warrior at home in his village laughed and played with his children and had hilarious times at festivals.

Other Indians from the Atlantic Ocean to the Mississippi River lived in constant fear of Iroquois raiding parties of swift, noiseless men who sneaked up on villages in the night and made off with prisoners or scalps or both. Yet these ruthless warriors are known in history as great peacemakers. The men who made our Constitution found inspiration in the Iroquois League, and the Iroquois were honored and respected by British, French, and American statesmen. George Washington called them "the Romans of the New World."

Who were these Iroquois? And where did they come from? We think that sometime between seven hundred and a thousand years ago, a number of Iroquoian tribes began to move north and east out of the warm, rich lowlands of the southern Mississippi. Although they started out from Mound Builder

Elm tree bark provided the walls and roofs of Iroquois longhouses and the shells of their canoes, except in the northernmost part of their hunting ground where they found birch bark.

Many families lived together in an Iroquois longhouse. Each family had its own screened-off double-decker bunk. A row of small cooking fires ran down the center of the long room.

country, nobody is sure whether they were themselves Mound Builders or simply hunters and raiders. Traveling by canoe and on foot, they pushed slowly up the Mississippi to the Ohio River and then on into strange country beyond—always looking for a good place to settle down and live. They may have been a backward people to begin with, but they quickly learned from the Mound Builders they met along the way. They learned how to farm and they collected their own supplies of seeds—along with corn-growing ceremonies and religious beliefs that went all the way back to the Mayans.

Still it was no easy thing to find a new homeland in which a group of tribes could settle and plant fields permanently. Mound Builders in one place, hunting tribes in another, already held the land wherever the Iroquois went. So their trek was one long, constant battle. The men had to be warriors and they had to fight very well if they were going to survive at all.

At last five of the Iroquois tribes found a home to their liking—the rich valleys of New York. More primitive tribes of Algonquins already lived there, but the Iroquois invaders were determined. They drove the Algonquins from their small wigwams and built in their place large, barnlike community houses called longhouses, in which several families lived. To protect their new villages, the Iroquois encircled them with solid log palisades. Then they went to work setting forest fires along the rivers and streams to clear the land, just the way the Mayans had done for hundreds of years in the jungle. After the big fires, they built small ones around the base of every tree that remained standing. With stone axes they hacked away at the trunk of the tree as fast as it charred and finally brought it tumbling to the ground. By this slow, laborious process they made acre after acre ready for planting corn, beans, and squash. At the same time war parties were regularly sent out to harass the Algonquins and drive them back.

The Iroquois were skillful, fearless, and energetic, and they intended to stay. Before long they had learned all there was to know about warfare in the dense, tangled forests, and the highest honors went to the men who were brave and successful in battle.

Now a strange thing happened. Fighting had become such a habit that the Iroquois often went on raids just to win honors. War, which began as a necessity, had become a sport. Teams of warriors went out from their villages looking for glory, just as football teams go out to play the teams of other colleges today.

While the men were off at war, winning fame and honors, the women raised the children and did the farming. Although the Iroquois were the greatest hunters in the eastern woodlands and they brought home deer, bear, and every kind of game, their mothers, wives, and grandmothers were the real providers and the real rulers, too. The women seldom held office. Instead, they did the actual choosing of the civil leaders, called sachems, and of the religious leaders, called Keepers of the Faith, who were in charge of the ceremonies. It sometimes happened, for example, that an ambitious grandmother would decide that a certain boy should one day be a sachem. Whether or not he ever held the post depended largely on the old lady's political skill. If she could persuade a majority of the other women, her choice would be theirs. To the men was left the privilege of selecting a warrior to hold the less important post of war chief.

From his boyhood on, an Iroquois warrior was schooled in the arts of self-discipline and physical fortitude. An Iroquois never cried out in pain or showed fear. Somewhat in the fashion of the Hopewell Mound Builders, he pulled out most of his hair and left only a scalp lock high on the top of his head as a kind of deliberate announcement: "I have made it easy for you to take my scalp—but just try to do it!" The scalp lock had a practical reason, too, for the forests were no place for long flowing hair that might get tangled in bushes or branches and slow down a stalking warrior.

Iroquois warriors maintained the most strenuous kind of training for years. Long-distance running was particularly important for they often needed to cover great distances in a hurry. Young men practiced trotting along the narrow woodland paths until some of them could actually cover a hundred miles in a day.

Boys and young men spent a great deal of time at sports of many kinds that helped them grow agile and tough. One ball game that was popular then and is still played today is lacrosse. During festivals and at other times, too, teams from different villages, or from opposite sides of one village, tried their strength and endurance in this rough-and-tumble contest. The game was long and players often got injured. It was no sport for cowards or weaklings.

Boys practiced using weapons, too—tomahawks, bows and arrows. They studied all the tricks of moving silently through the woods to prepare for making sneak attacks. With all this training and with honors waiting for every hero in battle, it was no wonder that young men were eager to go on the warpath. They didn't need much of

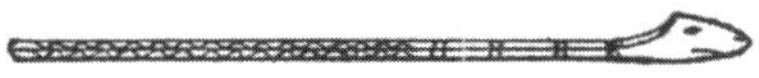

In winter men and boys competed in sliding a long rod called a snow snake (left) over the hard snow.

Young men hardened themselves for war and the hunt by playing the rough game of lacrosse.

an excuse. The emphasis on war was so great that the different Iroquois tribes often fought with each other as well as with the Algonquin tribes. Usually the fighting was done in swift surprise raids or sudden attacks from ambush rather than large-scale battles.

Still, Iroquois warriors often got killed, and villages that lost men needed a way of replacing them. So, instead of killing their enemies in battle, the Iroquois usually tried to capture as many as possible, just as the Mayans and other Central American Indians did. But the Iroquois wanted only the cream of the captives. A war prisoner had to prove that he was worth keeping alive. As a test of his courage and quickness he had to run the gantlet. This consisted of two rows of women and children facing each other and armed with sticks, whips, or clubs, between whom the captive had to dash as fast as he could, ducking blows and dodging like a halfback running through a broken field. If he arrived unscathed at the end of the gantlet, he was allowed to enter a longhouse where an old woman who had lost her own son in battle waited to adopt him. Never afterward would any member of the tribe harm him.

If a captive was weak or slow in running the gantlet, the Iroquois killed him. There was no room among them for any but the strong and the bold. But anyone who survived the test was so well treated that he almost always became a loyal member of his adopted tribe. In this way, the Iroquois replenished their strength in spite of constant warfare.

They had a practical reason for the gantlet, but there was more to the custom than that. It was a variation on the practice of human sacrifice that had come down from the Mayans. The Iroquois didn't draw blood from their captives or torture and kill them out of sheer cruelty. They were following an age-old religious custom. Like Mayans before them, they sacrificed things of value to show their gratitude to the gods, and the most precious thing of all was the blood of human life. To an Iroquois, running the gantlet was an honorable custom—quite as much as loving all children and being kind to his family.

One of the most dramatic Iroquois customs was the Jadigonsa or False Face Society. Like many Indians, the Iroquois believed that by donning the face of a particular animal or one representing an evil spirit or disease, they thereby had power over and could drive away a threatening calamity. And so they had the False Face Society, like a group of doctors, for the protection of the people.

The members of the society were medicine men, and no one was supposed to know who they were. If some member of the tribe had a particularly vivid dream about an animal or possibly something appearing to be an evil spirit, he reported it to one of the big men in the False Face Society. If his dream was significant enough to make him eligible, he was taken out to the woods to carve for himself a mask from the soft wood of a living basswood tree. According to Iroquois legend, a mask cut from the live tree is particularly powerful.

In the middle of the winter the Society held a purification rite, somewhat like our spring house cleaning. Wearing their grotesque masks and weird robes, the medicine men went into all the houses in the village. They opened all the doors, put out the fire in the hearth, and kindled a new one. They blew onto the heads of the dwellers the ashes of the old fire and departed, having driven out all the evil spirits for the year.

The False Face Society was common to all nations of the Iroquois League. While it is ancient in its origin and false faces were common among most of the American Indians, the Iroquois have no history of having slowly evolved this society over the years. They believed instead that it along with their ceremonial songs and dances were given to one of their ancestors by a supernatural being. In much the same

False Face masks.

way they explain the formation of the Iroquois League, which was comparatively recent and was unique in its conception and achievements.

An old legend, which may have a basis in fact, tells how the Onondaga, the Cayuga, the Mohawk, the Seneca, and the Oneida tribes banded together in the Iroquois League to keep the peace.

Once in the distant past, says the legend, there was an Onondaga named Hiawatha (not the one about whom Longfellow wrote), who saw how much better off all his people would be if peace prevailed throughout the woodlands. He suggested the idea to the powerful chief of his tribe, Atotarho, whose name means "the Tangled One." But Atotarho, a fierce tyrant, would not listen and implacably opposed all Hiawatha's efforts to promote his new idea.

So Hiawatha set out alone on a great pilgrimage, talking to people in all of the Iroquois tribes and trying to make them see the importance of peace. He went through deep forests, he canoed down dangerous rivers, he climbed steep mountains. Finally he talked to the chief of the Mohawks, Dekanawidah (meaning "Two-river-currents-flowing-together"), who not only listened to him but was able to plan exactly how a league of Indian tribes should work.

Together Hiawatha and Dekanawidah convinced four Iroquois tribes—the Cayugas, Mohawks, Senecas, and Oneidas—of the desirability of banding together for peace. Then they went to Atotarho and, since he was renowned as a great magician, persuaded him that joining this league would increase his reputation even more.

The sachems of the five tribes gathered at the head town of the Onondaga, where Dekanawidah instructed them to plant a tree, the Tree of Peace, whose branches would touch the clouds of heaven. Under it a fire must be kindled to burn forever, and there the sachems must always sit in harmony. The league was to be known as the Longhouse.

In the Longhouse the Mohawks, who were the easternmost tribe, were the Keepers of the Eastern Door, and the Senecas, far to the west, were the Keepers of the Western Door. They with the Onondagas, the Keepers of the Great Council Fire, were the stronger or elder brothers of the weaker Cayuga and Oneida tribes.

No Indians in the United States had a written language, but many tribes recorded events with pictures drawn on skins, bark, rock, or thin slabs of wood. The Iroquois pictograph above tells the story of a raid in which one man armed with bow and arrows was killed (the headless figure) and three persons were captured—a man with a gun, a woman (note the skirt), and a man with a tomahawk.

A warrior scalped a man and a woman.

A hunter killed three does.

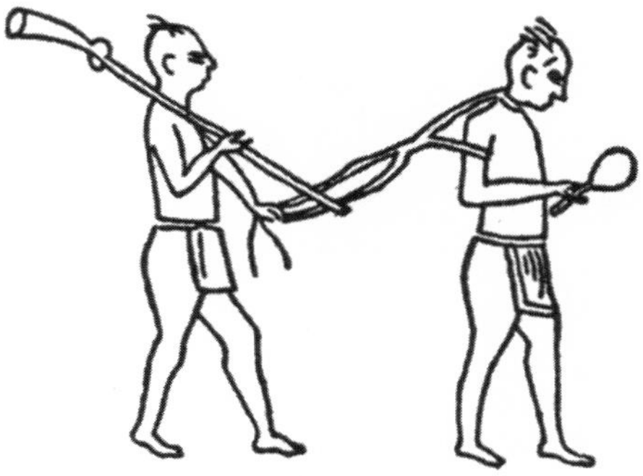

A warrior captured one enemy.

Most tribes were divided into clans of people who claimed descent from a common ancestor. Very often the ancestor was believed to be an animal. Among the Iroquois and many other groups descent in clans was traced through the mother rather than the father. Each clan had its own symbol (or totem) representing the animal ancestor. These old drawings show some of the Iroquois clan totems: plover, turtle, beaver, wolf, deer, bear.

However legendary Hiawatha or Dekanawidah may have been, the Iroquois League itself was very real. At the very time the death cult was sweeping the Mound Builders and their culture was coming to an end, the Iroquois were finding a way of preserving and expanding their life.

Near the end of the sixteenth century the wiser sachems in some of the Iroquois tribes began to realize that their people would be much better off if an end were put to the wars they were constantly waging.

First, of course, fighting among the Iroquois had to stop. Later they could make peace with the Algonquins and other outsiders.

And so about the year 1600 the Onondaga, the Cayuga, the Mohawk, the Seneca, and the Oneida tribes did get together and succeeded in creating a stronger political organization than any other Indians north of Mexico ever achieved. Their influence spread far beyond the forests of New York. To the pioneers and to the Indians of other tribes the Iroquois capital at Onondaga was, up until the nineteenth century, one of the most important towns in the New World.

In order to settle the disputes that did arise among themselves, or with the Algonquins and later with the white man, the League set up a council of fifty sachems, who were selected by the older women in each of the five tribes. The sachems were summoned for meetings by swift runners who sped over the hundreds of miles of narrow forest trails. They gathered in the main Onondaga town by the embers of the council fire. Naturally there was a great deal of talk at their meetings, and in time Iroquois leaders became marvelous orators, among the world's greatest in fact. Words that still seem to have magic in them when you read them today streamed from the lips of these proud men famed for their silence in the face of danger.

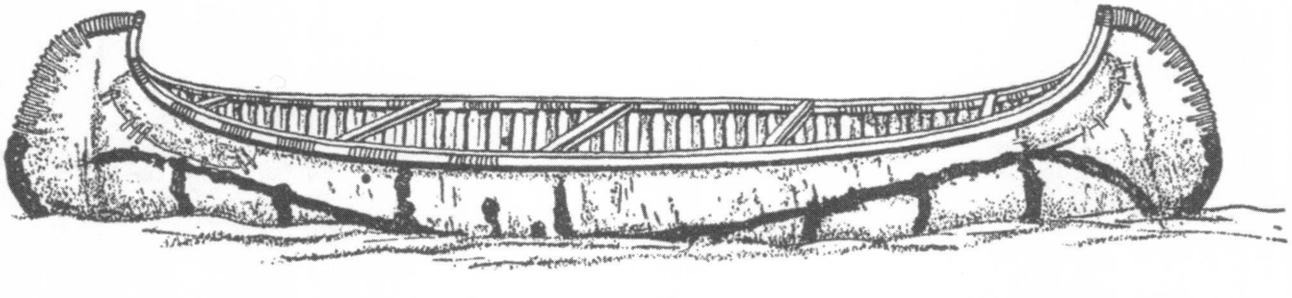

Where bark could be removed from trees in large sheets, Indians made it into light, graceful canoes. Birch trees abounded in the northern forests— and so did birch bark canoes. Elm bark was the best material that could be found farther south. Throughout the southern states Indians shaped whole tree trunks into dugout canoes.

One of the masterpieces of Iroquois oratory was spoken by John Logan or Tahgahjute, who was half Cayuga and half French, at the peace council following Lord Dunmore's War in 1774:

> I appeal to any white man to say if he ever entered Logan's cabin hungry and he gave him not meat. If ever he came cold and naked and he clothed him not. During the course of the last long and bloody war, Logan remained idle in his cabin, an advocate for peace. Such was my love for the whites that my countrymen pointed as they passed and said, "Logan is the friend of the white man." I had even thought to have lived with you but for the injuries of one man, Colonel Cressap, who last spring, in cold blood and unprovoked, murdered all the relations of Logan not even sparing my women and children. There runs not a drop of my blood in the veins of any living creature. This called on me for revenge. I have sought it. I have killed many. I have fully glutted my vengeance. For my countrymen I rejoice at the beams of peace, but do not harbor a thought that mine is the joy of fear. Logan never felt fear! He will not turn on his heel to save his life. Who is there to mourn for Logan? Not one.

This United Nations in the forest was very much like the Security Council of the United Nations today. As Dekanawidah had advised them, discussion went on until all the sachems agreed, or else there was no decision. All their agreements had to be unanimous, and they did agree well enough so that peace spread throughout the woodlands.

The sachems had to keep a record of every treaty or agreement they made. Since they had no written language, they devised—or, as legend has it, Hiawatha gave to them before ascending to heaven in his white birch bark canoe—something that was a little like tying a string around your finger to remind you of something. They strung together white and blue shells called wampum and made them into belts. Each design in

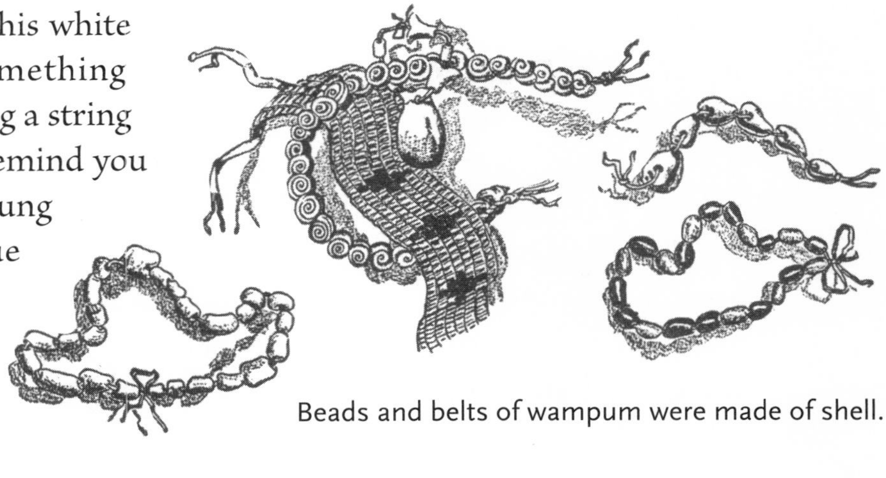

Beads and belts of wampum were made of shell.

a belt stood for a part of a treaty or agreement. A sachem was appointed Keeper of the Wampum, whose job it was to memorize every decision that the council of sachems made, using the wampum designs to jog his memory.

As the years went on, the Keeper of the Wampum had many belts in his care. And, of course, he had to store away in his mind all the agreements that they represented.

The Five, and later Six Nations—when the Tuscaroras joined them in the eighteenth century—were each represented by strings of purple wampum, tied together at one end and decorated with tufts of red cloth at the other. The council was opened when these strings were laid in a circle and it was adjourned when they were taken up. When a sachem wanted to speak, he picked up the bunch belonging to his tribe and held it as long as he spoke. The Iroquois were very solemn at their meetings and an orator was seldom interrupted before he put down his string of wampum.

More and more leaders from all over the woodlands sat down and smoked the sacred calumet or peace pipe with the fifty Iroquois sachems. Peace among the Indians spread over more and more territory. Then the white man came, and trouble started all over again.

The English and the French fought each other in order to win control of the new continent. They drew the Indians into their fight—some on the English side and some on the French. Indians on both sides received guns, sharp metal tomahawks, and steel knives. During the American Revolution, Englishmen paid warriors in several Iroquois tribes to take the scalps of colonists. In Pennsylvania and other places, rewards were offered to white men for taking Iroquois scalps. In the end, the Iroquois League was destroyed by white men before it could realize its goal of one great peaceful government over all Indians.

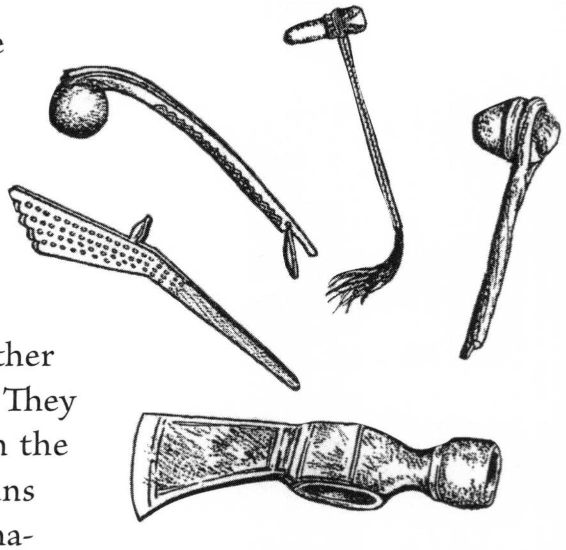

War clubs, often called tomahawks, had many forms. White traders introduced a metal tomahawk shaped like a hatchet that could also be used as a tobacco pipe.

But an important Iroquois idea lived on. The men who helped create the United States of America knew the Iroquois and the strength of their

League. Washington and Jefferson knew it at first hand, and they realized what an impressive human achievement it represented. Benjamin Franklin, says Carl Van Doren, "admired the Iroquois confederation, and plainly had it in mind in his earliest discussion of the need for a union among the colonies." Certainly our form of government has its roots in the achievements of these first Americans as well as in the ideas that came from Europe.

Chapter Eight

Mystery Dogs

ABOUT THREE HUNDRED and fifty years ago a large new animal appeared in Pueblo land. Hunting tribes all around regarded it eagerly, for here was meat, and plenty of it. The mysterious new animals were bigger than deer, but many of them seemed as tame as dogs. They stayed around the homes of the Spaniards who had moved into the area, just the way dogs stayed around Indian homes. Before long Indians were calling these new animals "mystery dogs." They were horses, of course—tough Arab horses accustomed to living in a dry land where forage was scarce.

At first, the hunting Navahos, Apaches, Comanches, and Utes ate horsemeat whenever they could get it. Often they made raids on Spanish ranches and ran off with the animals. Sometimes the Spaniards traded decrepit old nags to the hunters in the hope of discouraging raids. But they were careful not to let the Pueblo Indians own horses or even ride them, for they were trying to turn the Pueblos into slaves, and slaves on horseback were much too likely to develop ideas of their own about freedom.

However, in spite of these precautions, in 1680 the Pueblos rose in revolt and drove out the Spaniards. This first American Revolution succeeded in keeping the foreign rulers away from the Southwest for twelve years. But their horses stayed behind. By now the Pueblos who had served as stable boys knew all the secrets of saddles, bridles, and lariats. They had watched their Spanish masters break and ride horses. They had even learned to ride when their masters' backs were turned. During their twelve years of freedom, the Pueblos became horse traders. Since they weren't travelers they had little use for the "mystery dogs" themselves and preferred the Spaniards' small burros for carrying wood and bags of grain. But the Pueblos could and did trade to other Indians both horses and their knowledge of horsemanship. They taught the hunting tribes that the animals were more valuable alive than dead, for a man in the saddle could kill much more food than a man on foot. Families with horses could move a great deal farther and faster in search of game.

Now the "mystery dogs" began to pass quickly from tribe to tribe, all the way to the Great Plains and north along the Rocky Mountains. Bands of wild horses spread, too. Shoshoni Indians in Wyoming and up into Idaho learned to ride. They handed on their knowledge to tribes in the northern part of the plains.

A whole new kind of Indian life began. Everything speeded up. Those who had once led a slow, settled life now traveled restlessly. Poor Indians became rich. Most dramatic of all was the story of how horses changed a tired, defeated people into conquerors of the plains. They were the people we call the Sioux. Their own name for themselves was Lakota or Dakota (depending on the regional dialect), which means "friendly." The word Sioux is a North American French version of an Iroquis word meaning "speaker of a foreign language."

While the horse was traveling up from Pueblo land, the Lakota were moving westward out of the woods and lake country of Minnesota. The Ojibways to the east, having obtained guns and ammunition from the white man, had overwhelmed the Lakota who still used only bows and arrows. In the end, the Lakota had had to leave their farms and woodland hunting grounds behind them.

When the homeless refugees reached the great prairie country, they found that much of their old knowledge was useless. Around them lay millions of acres covered with grass instead of trees. Farming on this dry land had to be done in ways they had never learned. Vast herds of buffalo fed on the sea of grass, but men on foot could not kill enough of the fast-moving beasts to keep their families alive the year round. The tattered, wretched bands of Sioux plodded along, looking for better country. The women carried babies or big bundles on their backs. Dogs carried smaller bundles which rested on a device called a *travois*—two poles strapped over the dog's shoulders and dragging out behind.

Finally they reached the Missouri River. In their weariness and discouragement, the Sioux looked at first with amazement and then with growing hope at the sight they beheld on the banks of the great river. There, near the earth lodges of a strange tribe, the Arikara, big animals were pulling very heavy loads on travois. They could see men racing across the open land on the backs of the same kind of animal.

The Lakota had precious little to offer in trade, but they managed to get a few horses from the Arikara. Using these, they got more and more by stealing from every other Plains tribe. In a very short time the ragged refugees had become wealthy and powerful.

Along with their horses the Lakota picked up something else from the Indians they met on the plains—a means of communication. Before the Sioux came, many other tribes with horses had moved into the plains from every direction. Often when strange tribes met, they wanted to trade with each other or exchange news. But their languages were different, and most people spoke only their own. So these plainsmen worked out an intricate sign language which spread throughout the prairie country—two thousand miles north and south and almost five hundred miles east and west. It was such an excellent means of communication that anyone could use it, whether he was a Cheyenne or a Comanche, a Kiowa or a Blackfoot, an Arapaho or a Crow.

Indians made the signs almost entirely with their hands, and they could "talk" nearly as fast as they could in spoken words. The Sioux were quick to learn the international language, just as they were quick to take up many other customs of the Plains Indians they met.

No Lakota even thought of farming now. A few men on horseback, armed with bows and arrows, could bring down more food in a day than a whole village of women could get out of the soil in a summer of hard work. With tepees made of buffalo hide, the Sioux were free to wander far and wide on the prairie—and to be comfortable wherever they went.

In the spring, they watched for the endless herds of buffalo to move northward, following the grass as it turned green. Scouts rode out from the camps, constantly on the lookout. When a scout caught sight of the buffalo, he sent word to camp with almost telegraphic speed. He simply ran back and forth

Bear

Deer

Defy

Lie

True

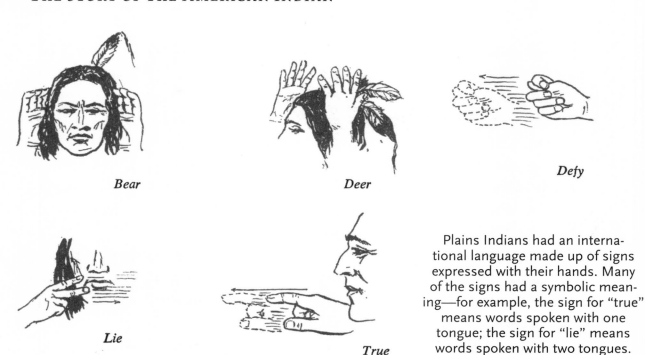

Plains Indians had an international language made up of signs expressed with their hands. Many of the signs had a symbolic meaning—for example, the sign for "true" means words spoken with one tongue; the sign for "lie" means words spoken with two tongues.

on the top of a rise or hill. Another scout, nearer camp, was watching for just this signal. When he saw it he, too, ran back and forth on a hilltop. In a matter of minutes the news about the herd had crossed many miles.

The village immediately came to life. Athletic young hunters ran for their favorite horses that were tethered nearby and assembled to follow the directions of the hunt leader. This was no haphazard dash, with each man looking out for himself. It was a community effort in which every person knew his place and what was expected of him.

While the hunters organized and set off under their leader, the women rolled up the great tepee covers and tied the tepee poles onto the horses to serve as travois. Buffalo robes and skin containers holding all the household goods were packed on the travois poles. Small children sat on top of the bundles, while mothers carried babies in cradle boards, either slung on their backs or hanging from their saddles. With the horses all rounded up and packed,

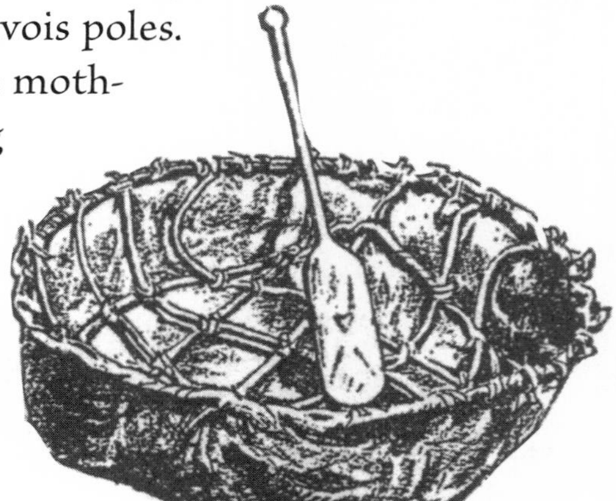

For transporting their goods across large rivers, Plains Indians made circular boats, called bull boats, of buffalo skin. After the crossing, the skin could be removed and loaded onto a travois. Here is an empty bull boat with a paddle.

the whole village started out, following the tracks of the men.

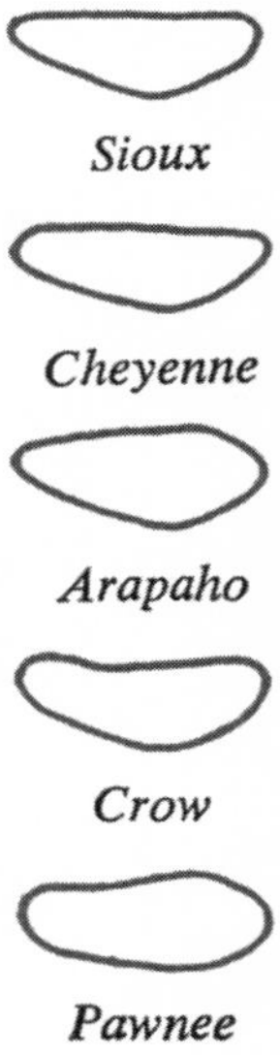

Indian boys were trained to be experts at tracking. Often they could tell what tribe a person belonged to by the shape of the footprint he left. The outline of the moccasin sole was one clue. At the right, from top to bottom, are moccasin soles of the Sioux, Cheyenne, Arapaho, Crow, and Pawnee.

Far out ahead of the women, the hunt leader talked to the scouts and studied the land before he made a plan of attack. If he found a cliff or a bluff nearby, he might decide to stampede the animals over it. That was the old-fashioned way—and the easiest. Or the leader might plan to surprise the animals out in the open, for now that the Lakota had horses, it was no problem to dash up to the herd and shoot them with their powerful bows.

Hunters always rode light—no saddle, no clothes except a breechcloth and moccasins, not even a feather in their hair. Many did without quivers, simply holding their arrows in their hands. Shooting was quicker that way.

Keeping behind low hills, the hunters moved in as close to the herd as possible. Some of them said that long running made the buffalo meat tough, and it certainly tired the horses. Men who had brought extra horses with them changed mounts behind the last sheltering rise of land. Then, at their leader's signal, they galloped as fast as their swift little ponies could carry them, straight toward the grazing beasts.

With a terrible thunder of hoofs, the buffalo ran and kicked up a curtain of dust that at first hid them from sight. But, as the horses gained on them, each man burst out ahead of the dust and chose his target. One aimed at a tough old bull whose hide would be best for making a new shield. Many selected cows whose meat would be tender and whose hides made the best tepees. A boy on his first hunt would try for a calf.

The rider pounded his heels into the horse's sides, urging him on faster and faster. Then, when the horse realized which animal his rider was after, he dodged and shifted so that he could move close up to that buffalo's right side. Leaning forward to get as close to the running target as possible, the hunter aimed his arrow just behind the ribs. A good shot went to the heart and sent the buffalo stumbling to its knees. Boys with middling strength often aimed at the hip joint. A wound there made the animal sit down, and another shot or two would kill it. Then horse and rider would be off after another target.

Both knew it was not safe to get surrounded by the terrified herd or to get even close to an animal that seemed to be watching its pursuers. Buffalo were quick and immensely strong. One swift gouge of a bull's horns could rip through a horse and man and toss them to one side.

One by one as the riders used up their arrows, they slowed down. They had killed enough, and it was no pleasure to waste the precious buffalo.

Looking back, they could see shaggy brown-black bodies scattered through the grass. Here and there lay a little red calf, brought down by boys who had won their first honors as hunters. Like their fathers,' their own specially marked arrows showed which calves they had killed.

Plains Indian warriors decorated their buffalo bull hide shields with feathers and with paintings having personal religious significance.

The buffalo were butchered on the spot, and each hunter claimed the best parts of the animals he had shot. The rest was divided back at camp, according to tribal law so that the poor and sick would get their share.

By the time the hunters returned to camp, the women had set up the tepees in a circle beside whatever stream they found nearest the hunting ground. And they did not just put the tepees wherever they felt like it. There were definite rules about their arrangement, and each woman knew exactly where her tepee belonged.

That night they prepared fresh meat to eat, tender buffalo tongues and the juicy hump. The rest—tons and tons of it—had to be preserved. Now the women would be busy for days, putting every bit of the buffalo to good use to provide all the tribe would need for food, shelter, clothes, and tools for a long time to come.

Sioux women, like all women of the plains, sliced the meat into thin sheets and dried it in the sun. This was jerky which would keep a long time. But pemmican would keep even longer—sometimes for a year. To make it, the women pounded jerky into a fine powder, which they mixed with dried berries and animal fat. The result was very like the mincemeat we make into pies. Finally they "canned" the pemmican by putting it into skin containers which they sealed with grease to keep out the air.

Dozens of hides remained after a big hunt. The women scraped the hair off some and got them ready

Bear design on a Mandan shield.

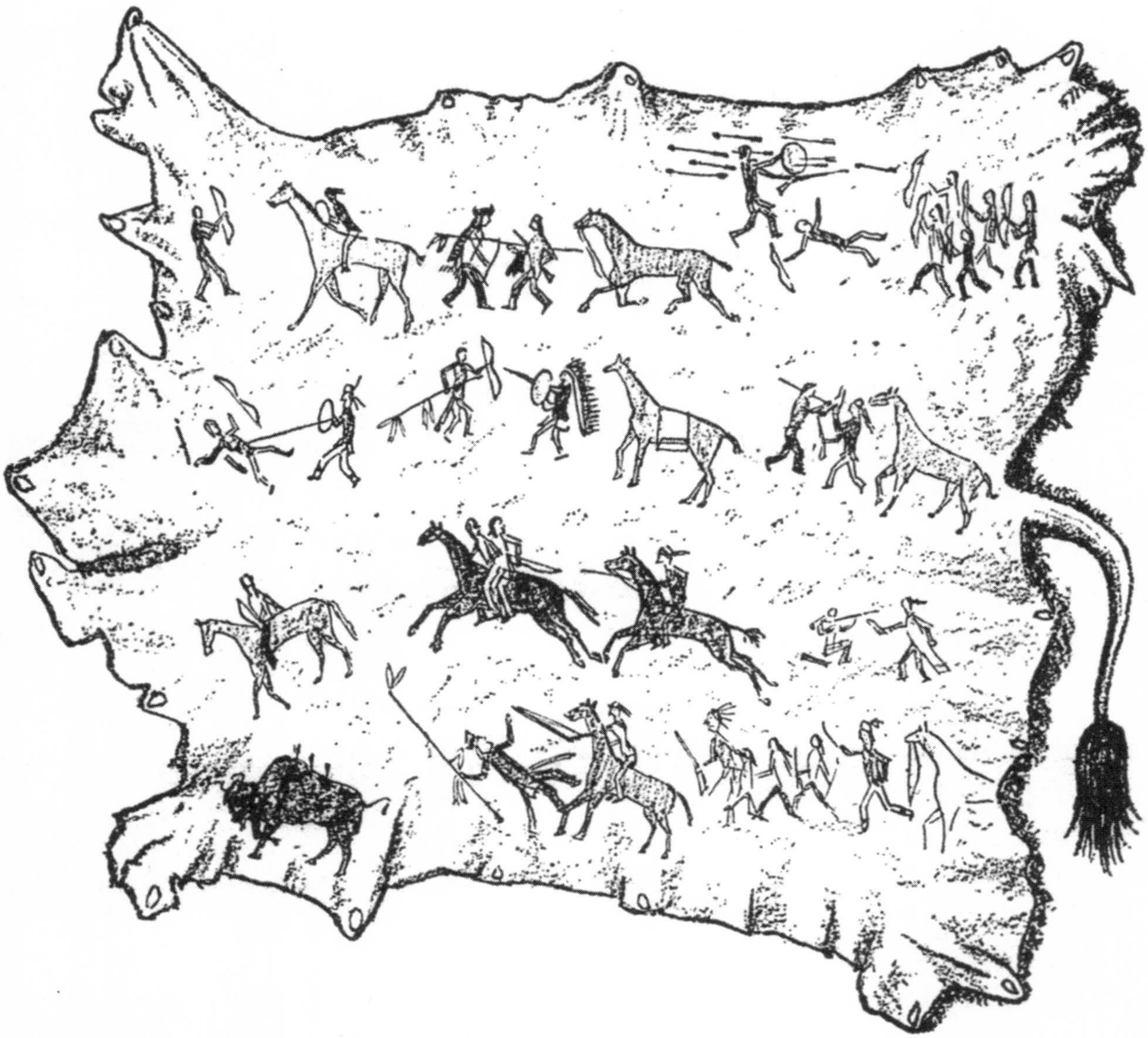

The Shoshoni chief Washakie, like many Indians in and around the Great Plains, painted on a whole buffalo skin the record of some of his exploits.

- In the top row, the first drawing shows Washakie meeting a Sioux whom he killed. Next Washakie (right) is meeting a Sioux chief. The last picture tells that Washakie (left) met a band of Blackfeet, killed one of them, and was himself wounded in the nose by an arrow.
- The second line shows Washakie after running a spear through a Blackfoot; in war bonnet fighting a Cheyenne; and holding his horse, face to face with a Sioux, whom he first struck with a six-shooter, then shot with a rifle.
- The third row tells that Washakie met two Utes on horseback who were armed with bows and arrows. He shot and killed them both. A Blackfoot, hiding under a rock shot at Washakie, but missed. Washakie then fired and killed the Blackfoot.
- The fourth row tells how a long time ago Washakie killed a buffalo with three arrows; how he (on horseback) met the brother of Crazy Horse; how he met four Blackfeet, got off his horse, chased the four, and killed them all.

A shield was so hard and thick that it gave real protection from arrows, but it proved useless against the white man's bullets.

for sewing into new tepee covers and boxes, clothes, moccasin soles, and big envelopelike containers. To tan the hides, they smeared the brains of the buffalo on the fresh skins and rolled them up. Chemicals in the brains helped make the thick hide soft and pliable. Often the hair was left on the hide of a buffalo killed in winter, when it was long and shaggy and made the warmest bed coverings or robes to wear in the bitter prairie blizzards.

Not a bit of the buffalo went to waste. Horns were shaped into spoons, containers, and decorations for medicine men's headdresses. The big shoulder blades became shovels for digging storage pits in the earth. Splinters of bone were used as awls. Some pieces of bone were fashioned into arrowheads. Knives would come from ribs. The men saved dewclaws and some of the hoofs for the rattles they used in ceremonies. Hoofs were boiled into glue for sticking feathers onto arrows. Big tendons cut loose from the hind legs would be dried and pounded into slender but strong threads. Strips of rawhide made bindings that held things together as tightly as if they had been clamped in iron. Ropes would be twisted out of the long hair that grew on the buffalo's head and shoulders. The stomachs were made into pots or bags. Indians found even the insides, as well as the meat, nutritious.

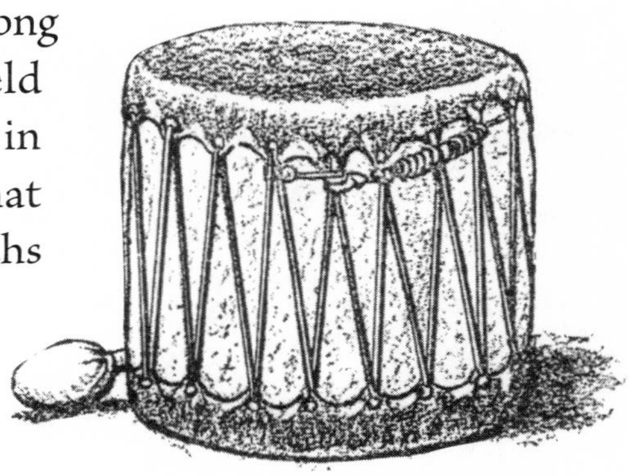

A drum made of buffalo skin.

The Lakota were so dependent on buffalo—and there were so many of these shaggy, humpbacked animals—that their life naturally centered around this apparently endless source of wealth. White Buffalo Calf Woman was an important figure in Lakota religion, and the Buffalo Dance was an important ritual performed before a hunt. A famous traveler of the nineteenth century, George Catlin, who both painted and wrote about the Indians, has this lively description of a masked Buffalo Dance in a village of the Mandans, who were related to the Sioux:

> My ears have been almost continually ringing since I came here, with the din of yelping and beating of the drums; but I have for

several days been particularly engrossed, and my senses almost confounded with the stamping, and grunting, and bellowing of the buffalo dance. . . .

Every man in the Mandan village is obliged by a village regulation to keep the mask of the buffalo hanging on a post at the head of his bed, which he can use on his head whenever he is called upon by the chiefs to dance for the coming of the buffaloes. The mask is put over the head, and generally has a strip of skin hanging to it, which, passing down over the back of the dancer, is dragging on the ground. When one becomes fatigued of the exercise, he signifies it by bending quite forward, and sinking his body toward the ground; when another draws a bow upon him and hits him with a blunt arrow, he falls like a buffalo—is seized by the bystanders, who drag him out of the ring by the heels, brandishing their knives about him; and having gone through the motions of skinning and cutting him up,

Older men taught boys ceremonial songs and dances. Note the buffalo skin backrest the man is leaning against, and his ceremonial pipe. In the background a woman prepares a new buffalo skin.

they let him off, and his place is at once supplied by another, who dances into the ring with his mask on; and by the taking of places, the scene is easily kept up night and day.

As the Lakota grew richer on the immense herds of buffalo, they held great Give Away Feasts. Men often gave away everything they owned at one of these big affairs—all their buffalo robes, their fine buckskin clothing decorated with porcupine quills, bags full of pemmican, bows and arrows, and, of course, horses which were the real measure of wealth. Important people got special gifts. Enemies were given things to make them more friendly. Relatives all received presents, and a man always passed around useful things for the old and the sick and the poor. It often happened that the host at a Give Away Feast slept with his family under the stars after it was over. Even his tepee was gone.

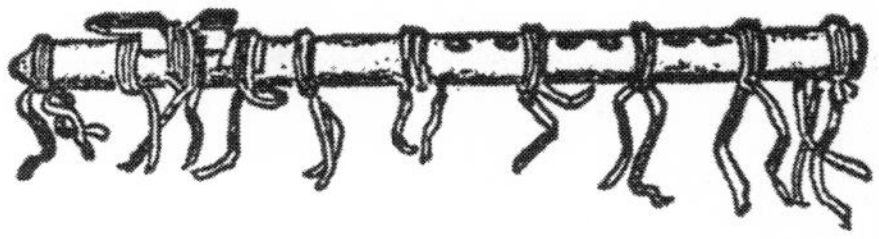

In various places Indians added the eerie wail of flutes to the rhythmic beat of drums at ceremonies. Sometimes a young man also played the flute when he went courting. This flute was made by the Kiowas, one of the Plains tribes.

Next day his guests showed their gratitude for his generosity. Horses appeared. Last night's guests brought new weapons and food. A fine tepee rose in place of the one that had been given away.

Indians had always shared when times were difficult. Now in good times the Lakota, and other tribes that were prospering because they had horses, made a spectacle of sharing. What had once been a necessity was now a way of having fun and of showing off. Since there was more than enough food to go around, the giver never suffered.

Another custom changed when the Lakota became horsemen and buffalo hunters. They had always held ceremonies in honor of the sun, but now they had a great Sun Dance celebration every summer in honor of the Great Unseen Spirit who they believed was the source of all their rich new life. During the rest of the year, the Lakota hunted and lived in separate bands. At Sun Dance time, all the bands assembled for one big tribal get-together. Young people held social dances; families gathered for reunions. People traded and feasted and played games. And some young men always took this occasion to carry out vows that they would endure tortures during the Sun Dance itself. First, sharp sticks were pushed under the skin of their chests or backs. Then the sticks were tied by long ropes to a pole. As the men danced, they jerked against the ropes until the skin gave way and they were freed.

Only the bravest could stand such pain without showing a sign of sufferings but many Lakota men had scars to prove that they had gone through the ceremony. Long training lay behind their ability to endure pain. From their earliest years they practiced running, wrestling in matches in which many boys took part at once, swimming in ice-cold water, and going without food for long periods of time.

All this training helped them to become strong hunters who could endure great hardship, and it made tough fighters of them, too. The Lakota became the most celebrated and the most feared of all the warrior nations on the plains. When they first reached prairie country, they had to fight extra fiercely because they were latecomers in the hunt for buffalo. Now that they had won their place on the plains, they kept on fighting just for the fun of it. As the Iroquois had done before them, the Lakota men became full-time warriors. They could do so because they had plenty of time and there was usually a good supply of food in their lodges. Like the Iroquois, too, the Lakota went on raids to win honors rather than to kill enemies. It was a high honor to come home safe from a raid with a new string of horses. The man with the most horses was obviously the bravest and best horse thief—a man to be looked up to. The Iroquois brought back human prisoners to strengthen their own tribe, but horses were vastly more important to the Lakota than captives, which they seldom took and never tortured.

The Lakota felt that it was a much greater honor to touch an enemy than to kill or to scalp him. They carried into battle special sticks, which we call "coup" sticks. When a Lakota touched an enemy with the stick, he said he "counted coup." They considered that any halfway decent bowman could shoot his foe from a distance and be fairly safe. But it took great courage indeed to dash up to a living enemy in the heat of battle, hit him with the stick, and get away alive. By the same reasoning, it sometimes took even greater courage to touch a dead foe. His friends were sure to be protecting his body and to use all their skill with bow and arrow, lance, or war club in doing so.

Moreover, a Lakota could not count coup unless he had witnesses. According to the rules, he had to call out loudly, "I perform the brave deed of counting coup upon this man who is brave among our enemies." This public announcement increased his danger, of course, and many a warrior fell as he tried to escape afterward. But if he did come back safely, he could be sure that everybody in his village would know what he had done. His witnesses told the official announcer, who then went through the village shouting praises of his bravery. From that day on, he could retell the adventure at ceremonies and boast about it—as long as he didn't embroider the tale. The witnesses were always there to see that he kept his story in line with the facts. And as a permanent reminder of his deed he was entitled to wear an eagle feather.

The Lakota worked out a whole system of wearing and marking their eagle feathers to show just which degree of courage a man had shown in battle. If he had counted coup and got away unwounded, he could wear the feather upright. If he had been wounded, the feather sloped backward. A round mark on the feather meant he had killed his enemy. If the feather was painted red and had a notch in it, the wearer had taken a scalp. A warrior won the right to wear the big-feathered war bonnet after he had done ten brave deeds in battle. Only the greatest leaders were allowed to wear bonnets with two long streamers of eagle feathers down their backs.

In the beginning, only the heroes among the Plains Indians wore the great eagle-feather war bonnets. Later other tribes borrowed the headdress and used it merely as a decoration.

Preparing for brave deeds in battle was not merely a matter of long practice in enduring hardships. Each warrior had to have his own "medicine"—that is, the protection of strong spirits who would bring him luck and protect him from harm. As every Lakota boy approached young manhood, he went off alone to fast and pray, sometimes for days, until he had a dream. Then he went to the medicine man who told him what the dream meant. Much of his life afterward depended on the interpretation of the dream. If it showed that he had strong medicine, he could be sure that if he worked hard, he would do great things. Sometimes a boy would have no dreams at all. He was sure he was doomed to failure—he felt he could never do anything at all. And he usually didn't.

But the failures and weaklings among the Lakota were exceptions. The white men who first met these horsemen of the plains were impressed with their dignity and courage and honesty. Still, these virtues were not enough. The life the Lakota had built around the buffalo disappeared as suddenly as it had begun.

A Plains Indian's headdress.

Up to the middle of the nineteenth century the Lakota were the strongest and most prosperous Indians on the plains. They possessed the huge hunting ground of the Black Hills of the Dakotas, known as Paha Sapa or Mountains-That-Are-Black. And they had either conquered or driven away their rivals until they controlled the vast lands west of the Missouri and south of the Yellowstone River to the Platte.

Then the railroad came, and with it professional hunters with modern guns who slaughtered the buffalo by the millions. The Lakota protested, and the American government promised to encroach no more on Sioux territory. Then in 1874 gold was discovered in the Black Hills, and the Indians found that the white man's promises were spoken with a forked tongue. For soldiers now came to drive the Sioux out and to make way for the onrush of white settlers and gold seekers.

The chiefs of the Sioux tribes, determined to resist the white man, gathered under the leadership of the great Hunkpapa medicine man, Sitting Bull, and the Oglala war chief, Crazy Horse. On June 26, 1876, the Sioux won the last great battle of the Indians against the white man in the famous Battle of the Little Big Horn, when they wiped out Custer and his men.

Just as the arrival of the horse brought a burst of new life to the Great Plains, so the arrival of the "Iron Horse" meant another and even greater change. Dogs continued to drag travois in the old way, nevertheless.

The warriors fought bravely to keep their land, but in the end the white men won for they had better food and guns and they had cannon. In a few short years the life-giving buffalo were gone—and with them, all that had once had meaning for the Sioux. They now had to begin life anew, as farmers and ranch hands, on reservations that were only a tiny part of the vast area over which they had once roamed freely. It is a tribute to their courage and their vitality that today there are more Sioux—Lakota, Santee Dakota, and Teton Dakota—than ever before in their history.

Cherokees on their reservation in North Carolina still do their ancient Eagle Dance
as part of a drama of Cherokee history performed for the public in July and August.

Chapter Nine

A New Nation— The Cherokee

By the 1820s one Indian tribe—the Cherokee—had made great strides toward taking its place among the civilized nations of the world. Ever since the Spaniard De Soto explored their wooded land among the Great Smoky Mountains nearly three hundred years before, the Cherokees had been learning from white men about new crops to grow, new methods of farming, new ways of making clothes and building homes. After the American Revolution they learned very rapidly indeed.

The Cherokee Nation—that was the tribe's official name, and for some time it dealt with the United States as would any other independent nation—sprawled over a huge territory in North Carolina, South Carolina, Georgia, Tennessee, and Alabama. All over the Nation in the 1820s farmers wearing their traditional turbans cultivated the soil with iron ploughs, and their wives made homespun cloth using their own spinning wheels and looms. Most families owned cattle and horses. Thousands of hogs fattened on acorns that fell on the hazy slopes of the highlands. Here and there Cherokee blacksmiths pounded out horseshoes or repaired iron tires for wagon wheels. Others operated ferries or gristmills.

The Cherokee Nation was rapidly becoming prosperous. But in the midst of their new comforts and achievements the Cherokees had more and more cause for worry. Year by year the territory of the Nation was growing smaller. The more prosperous the Cherokees became, the more land they lost to the whites.

One of the Cherokees who was deeply concerned for the future of his people was Sequoyah, a short, slender man who lived in what is now Tennessee. This quiet, obscure farmer, like other Cherokees, was reaching out and trying new things. Somehow he learned to be a silversmith, which no Cherokee had ever been before. He took silver coins that came from the British, the French, or the Americans and shaped them into ornaments, spoons, and spurs. He was clever with his hands and he soon added blacksmithing to his skills.

Sequoyah—from an actual portrait.

Sequoyah liked to paint, too. Without ever having seen the kind of brushes made of hair that white artists used, he invented them for himself and used them. The horses and buffalo he painted were better likenesses of animals than any Cherokee had ever made before.

All these activities, as well as hunting and farming, kept Sequoyah busy, but none of them solved a great problem that was on his mind. What made the white men so powerful, and how could his people learn their secret? How could the Cherokees become strong enough to keep white men from taking their land away?

Sequoyah, who was illiterate and who understood no language except Cherokee, finally decided he knew the answer. The white men had great power because they stored up all their knowledge in books. People who were dead could give all their wisdom to the living through written words. White men spoke back and forth to each other across great distances by using what Cherokees called "talking leaves." The ability to read and write made them stronger than the illiterate Indians.

Sequoyah was sure that if white men could invent a way of writing down their language, Cherokees could do the same. In 1809 when he was about thirty he decided to try.

Never before in all history had one man invented an entire method of reading and writing, but Sequoyah did not know this, and he started to work. At first he made thousands of drawings, or signs—one for each word. But there were so many words, and so many forms for each word, that he finally saw that this scheme would never work out. He couldn't even remember what all his own signs meant.

During the War of 1812, he interrupted his labors to join the American Army along with other Cherokees under General Andrew Jackson. He fought against the Creeks who were in the pay of the British, and apparently he was injured in battle. He limped ever afterward. But his injury did not stop his active mind from working. He persisted in trying to puzzle out a way to write.

By 1818, when he moved west in search of a new home in Arkansas, Sequoyah had made little progress toward taming the wild words of his mother tongue and getting them to do useful work on paper.

For years he had had to face the disapproval of the medicine men who thought he was trying to make magic. His neighbors thought the same, and so did his wife. Perhaps she was irked, too, because Sequoyah spent so much time making marks on pieces of bark and left so much of the farm work to her. At any rate she got the neighbors together one day and burned everything he had been working on for years.

"Well, now I must do it again," was all Sequoyah said, but the loss of his records made him start thinking along new lines. In Arkansas, where he supported his family by running a small trading post, a blacksmith shop, and a salt works, he made sure he had peace in which to study. He built a separate log cabin for himself out of earshot of his scolding wife.

One day it occurred to him that he might make a separate symbol for each syllable in the Cherokee language. By listening carefully he found that all the words could be made out of different combinations of eighty-six syllables. Now all he needed was a sign or symbol for each one. Actually, he was inventing a syllabary, not an alphabet.

First Sequoyah borrowed signs that he knew white men used in their writing. He had seen the letters of the English alphabet somewhere, some say in a spelling book he borrowed from a school, some say in a piece of old newspaper. He had no idea what the letters stood for, but it was convenient to use them to stand for the Cherokee sounds. He chose mainly the larger letters, the capitals in the English alphabet, and he turned some letters upside down. Then he drew many more of his own, until he had eighty-six in all. At last he could write down any word in the Cherokee language.

Inventing a syllabary was one thing—getting his people to accept and use it was another. Some scoffed; some muttered about magic when he told them what he had achieved. Clearly, he had to do something spectacular to prove the value of his invention.

Sequoyah taught his signs to his six-year-old daughter, Ayogu. Then, leaving her at home, he went to a court where a trial was going on. In court he wrote down exactly what happened. Later, in the presence of several chiefs he asked Ayogu to read what he had written, and she did. To the chiefs this demonstration meant only that there was magic at work somehow, and they didn't like it.

Still, one of them, Big Rattling Gourd, was troubled. Next day he came to Sequoyah and said, "I couldn't sleep last night. Yesterday by daylight what you did did not seem remarkable. But when night came, it was different. All night long I wondered at it and could not sleep. Sequoyah, show me those characters."

This was the break that Sequoyah needed and he was the happiest man in the world. Soon he arranged another public test. He asked the tribal leaders to select some young men to be taught his new method of communication. When the young men had learned the syllabary they

A player in this rough-and-tumble ball game had two sticks, each with a small net at the end. Originally the bustles, resembling horses' tails, were probably supposed to help the players run as swiftly as horses, which the Cherokees learned about very early from Spanish explorers. (From an old print by George Catlin.)

appeared before the chiefs to be examined. The chiefs dictated messages to some of the students and then other students who had not heard the dictation read what had been written down.

This test removed all doubt. Sequoyah had really invented "leaves" that could talk. The muttering about witchcraft ceased. The Cherokees in Arkansas gave Sequoyah a great feast and had a medal made in his honor.

All over the Cherokee part of Arkansas people covered their cabin walls and fences with writing. Sequoyah's invention was so simple that anyone could become completely literate in two or three days—sometimes in one. In 1824, Sequoyah himself set out to carry messages, written down in his syllabary, of course, back to the Cherokee Nation in the East. People in the Great Smokies accepted his invention with enormous enthusiasm. In no time everybody was learning. For the first time in the history of the world a whole nation became literate in a matter of months.

Cherokees, like other Indians in the South and like the Iroquois in the Northeast, used blowguns for hunting small game. The long tube was usually made of cane. The dart was a splinter of cane. The hunter wrapped one end of it with thistledown so that his breath had something to push against when he blew out the dart.

Now, Sequoyah thought, his invention could go to work for the Cherokees and give them the strength they needed to keep their lands from being taken from them by the whites.

On July 4, 1827, the Cherokees adopted a modern constitution modeled on the constitution of their neighboring republic, the United States of America. Seven months after that, they had a printing press and a newspaper, *The Cherokee Phoenix,* that ran the constitution serially in Cherokee, together with news both in English and in Cherokee. Here was a nation making faster progress toward civilization than any had ever made before.

But the progress had begun too late to give the Cherokees the strength and experience they needed in order to withstand the land-hungry whites. Gold was discovered in the Nation. A gold rush began and white men from Georgia

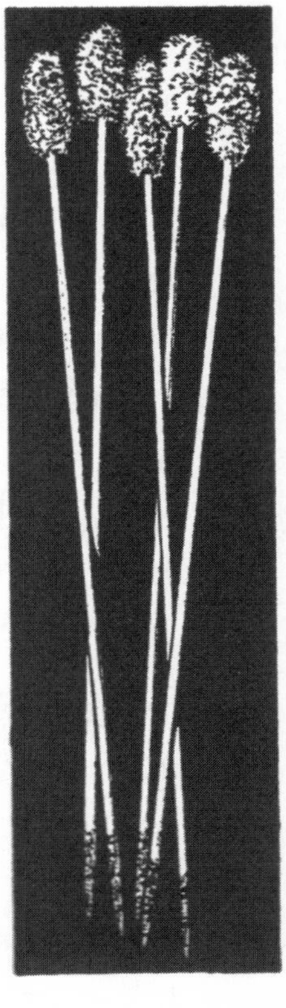

Darts the Cherokees used in their blowguns.

poured in by the thousands. Georgia claimed—and got—many thousands of acres of the Cherokee Nation.

Only a year later, in 1830, Congress in Washington passed a law ordering the removal of the Cherokees and other eastern tribes to land west of the Mississippi.

Eight years went by, however, and very few Cherokees moved. The people clung to their ancestral homes. By what right could any government order them to abandon all they had built up and loved? Nevertheless, the government in Washington did. In 1838 the United States Army began rounding up Cherokees, who made no effort to resist. Soldiers first built forts and stockades where they assembled their prisoners. Then they scoured the hills looking for the people to whom the hills belonged. Seventeen thousand Cherokees were forced to abandon their cabins and their farms to white settlers who followed the soldiers and paid little or nothing for all the wealth they took over. Cherokees who couldn't sell their hogs or their cattle had to leave them. They couldn't take along their looms or their blacksmith shops. Most of them couldn't take even their spinning wheels. Almost everything they had made and owned had to be left behind. Penniless and driven by soldiers, they were herded off to the West.

It's enough to say of this sad journey that four thousand Cherokees died of hunger, exposure, and disease along the way. It was literally a Trail of Tears and has been called that by the Cherokees ever since.

Just at the point where they were nearly ready to assume full responsibility as a nation among other nations, they suffered a tremendous setback, but the people themselves lived on. Today tens of thousands of men and women with Cherokee blood are living in Oklahoma. They are for the most part farmers and ranchers like any other citizens of that state. The number of old people who use the Cherokee language grows smaller each year. Sequoyah and his syllabary are only a memory of a different and perhaps more interesting kind of Cherokee life that might have grown up in Oklahoma.

In a different way, Cherokees lived on in the East. When the Army came to drive them from their homeland, many of them fled to the remotest parts of the mountains and stayed there, with caves for shelter and with only the food they could get by hunting.

One old man named Tsali had thought of joining those who fled to the hills, but in the end he and his sick wife and sons started out with the soldiers.

They had gone only a little way from home when a soldier grew annoyed with Tsali's wife who could not walk fast because she was ill. He tried to speed the old lady by threatening her with his bayonet.

This was too much for Tsali. He decided he and his family must escape, and he worked out a plan. Speaking Cherokee in a quiet conversational tone he told the plan to his sons as they marched along closely guarded by the armed white men. There were four soldiers and four sons. At a signal from Tsali each son was to disarm a soldier. Then the whole family would run away and hide in their beloved hills. Tsali warned his sons against killing their guards. He knew that would cause great trouble for all the Cherokee people. Escape was enough. Tsali would give the signal by falling and pretending to be hurt.

At a turn in the trail Tsali stumbled, fell, and cried out as if in pain. His sons seized the guns. Everything went according to plan, except that in the scuffle one gun went off accidentally and a soldier was killed.

Tsali and his family disappeared in the woods and no soldier could find them. The general in charge of the troops felt, however, that he could not let the death of his man go unpunished. He also had begun to realize that he would never be able to round up all the Cherokees who remained hidden in the mountains they knew so well. So he made an offer. He told a white trader who was trusted by the Cherokees that if Tsali and his sons surrendered for punishment, the Army would not bother any of the other Cherokees who had refused to move. The trader, William H. Thomas, believed the general would keep his word. He went straight to the cave in which Tsali was hiding and reported the general's offer. Tsali and his sons knew that if they returned with Thomas they would be executed for murder. But they decided this was not too great a sacrifice if their people could remain unmolested in their ancient homeland.

Tsali and his sons made their decision. They surrendered, and all except the youngest son fell before a firing squad. He returned to the hills and his people, and today three thousand Eastern Cherokees still live among the lovely mountains that their ancestors refused to leave.

These Northern Paiutes are collecting cones from an evergreen.

Chapter Ten

Seed-Gatherers Who Lived Where White Men Starved

AT THE TIME when Cherokees were reading, writing, governing themselves under a constitution, and managing farms in modern ways, some Indian tribes of the Far West still lived as if literacy and agriculture and even big-game hunting had never been invented. The art of making pottery was only dimly understood by these living relics of a very early stage in Indian history. Knowledge of basketry and the use of the bow and arrow marked the extent of their development. And the bow was of very little use to them, for they made their home in the great gameless basin that lies between the Sierra Nevada and the Rocky Mountains.

Rain seldom fell in this area, because the cool peaks of the Sierras drained all moisture out of the winds that came in from the Pacific. So, no corn grew in Nevada or in most of Utah or in a large part of southern California. Throughout all this dry region, patches of grass and clumps of leafy shrubs were scarce—too scarce to support deer, elk, bear, or buffalo. Horses were out of the question for general use until modern irrigation could produce hay. The only animals of any size that managed to survive were occasional bands of slender antelope. When white men first tried to cross this great waste, many of them died of starvation.

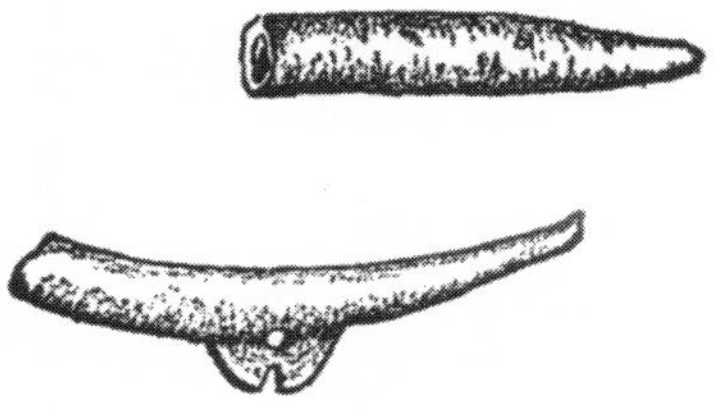

In southern California and in much of the Southwest, Indians smoked tobacco and herbs in pipes shaped like hollow tubes.

Yet in their bleak desert of sagebrush and sky, Indians lived by gleaning every wisp of scrawny vegetation. Out of the hopeless-looking plant life and the few small forms of hopping and crawling insect and animal life, they created tools, food, shelter, and clothes. With great ingenuity they worked out a remarkable way of existing. And they did so virtually alone and unaided. Few visitors bringing new ideas from other tribes ever ventured into their inhospitable land. They achieved whatever they did without stimulation from other people.

Whites gave all these people the name "Digger," because they saw them poking around in the dry earth with sticks, searching for edible roots or for the little stores of seeds that mice and other tiny animals had collected. Actually there were many different tribes of Diggers. The Northern Paiute of Nevada was typical.

Food was so scarce, and Paiutes had to move so often in search of it, that they lived in very small groups. They had almost no tribal organization and few group ceremonies or dances. But the members of the small groups did work together.

Each band had its own territory and knew from long experience exactly where every patch of vegetation grew, when the seeds would be ripe or the roots ready to eat. In spring people dug wild onions. Next they picked berries

Today Papagos manage to farm in the desert of southern Arizona. They build houses like this of adobe and brush.

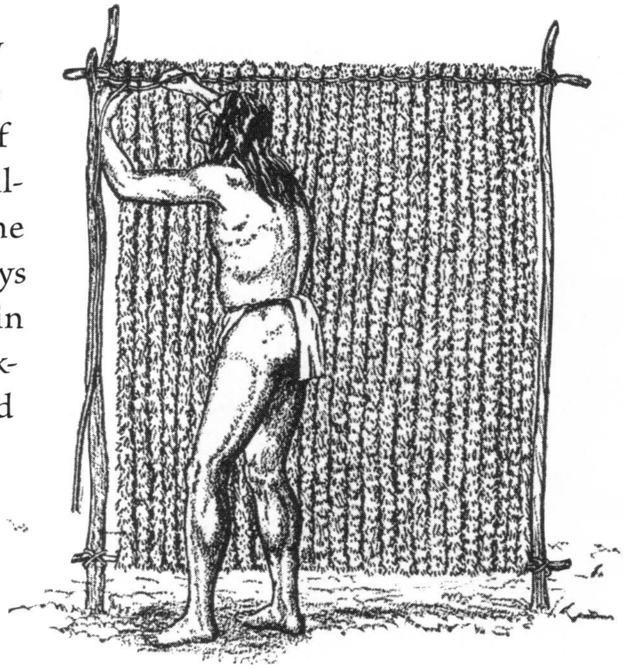

Paiutes wove light, warm blankets with long twisted strips of rabbit skin.

and the fruits of desert plants. Later they gathered the bulbs of a beautiful blue flower called the camas. Toward the end of summer there was a special harvest. Millions of crickets invaded the land. In the cold mornings when the insects were always sluggish, the women scooped them up in great handfuls and roasted them for breakfast on the coals of a fire. They also collected and roasted the larvae of various other insects. Dried ants were pounded into a kind of flour.

In autumn when plant seeds ripened, the Paiutes went out with fan-shaped beaters and shook tiny seeds from the dried heads of every single flower they could find, even clover, marigold, and primrose. Sunflower seeds were important, because they were larger than most. Where the low, ragged piñon pine trees grew, whole families gathered pine nuts in good years. Women took all these seeds and pounded them into flour which they cooked later to make a kind of soup or mush.

When the piñon nut crop was in, the men spent their time hunting for meat. In a land where green things were scarce, animals were scarcer. But the men poked long sticks into holes in the ground to bring out rats and ground squirrels. Sometimes they set snares for rabbits. Often a group of men worked together, stretching out a net, like an extra-long tennis net, and chasing rabbits into it. When the animals got stuck in the net, the hunters could kill them with sticks.

Men banded together, too, for antelope hunts, whenever they discovered a herd of the delicate, swift creatures. But a large kill was a rare thing, and there were never nearly enough skins to provide even the little clothing these Indians wore. Women made themselves skirts of

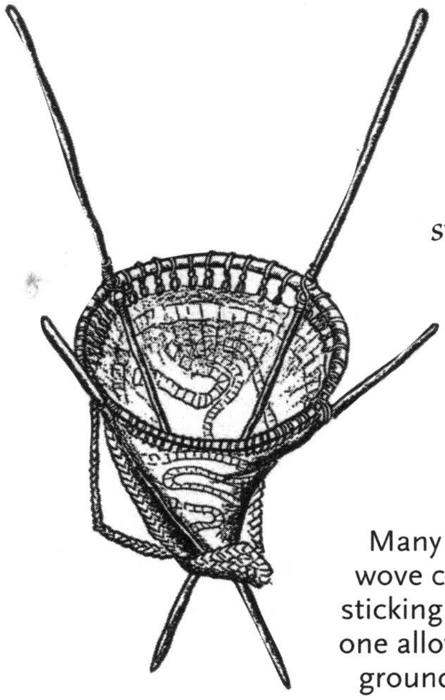

Many tribes in the desert areas wove carrying baskets. The poles sticking through the bottom of this one allow it to stand upright on the ground. The basket hung from a strap or tumpline across the head.

shredded sagebrush bark. A man might have a breechcloth made of skin, but if he wore sandals, they were fashioned from sagebrush bark. Their shelter, too, was supplied by this apparently useless plant. Over a framework of poles, the Paiutes piled brush for shade in summer. In winter, they covered the brush with mud.

Almost all the everyday utensils and tools were constructed from small twigs or reeds, blades of grass, or bits of fiber from bark. Working with only these materials, women wove everything from fanlike seed-beaters to cradle boards, cooking pots, and bowl-shaped hats for themselves. These basket caps gave no shade, but they protected their heads from being cut by the ropes, called "tumplines," that supported the large carrying baskets women bore on their backs. Baskets served as dishes, too. And reeds bundled together basket-fashion were rafts on which the Paiute men floated over the occasional ponds while hunting for waterfowl.

Blankets were even made by a kind of basketry-weaving process, although the material was rabbit skin or bird skin complete with feathers. Men always took the skin from a rabbit or a bird in one whole piece. Then they cut it, spiral fashion, so that it made one long strip. A twisted strip of skin made a thick

In many western tribes shinny was a popular game. Here Paiute women play with a special kind of ball, which was really two balls held together with a cord or strap.

yarnlike thread with fur or feathers sticking out on all sides. Blankets woven from the strips were very light and warm.

In such ways the Paiutes used the meager resources about them. They lived much as the basket maker ancestors of the cliff dwellers lived fifteen hundred or more years before, and they kept their own simple, peaceful way of life until the days of the Gold Rush in 1849. Then a whole new world, vastly different from their own, swirled around them so quickly that those who were not killed off had no time to learn how to adjust. The Paiutes and most of the other Diggers all but disappeared.

The ones who remain today live near their former food gathering grounds, where some of them work on the ranches and farms that modern science has made possible in their arid land.

This Haida ceremonial canoe from Alaska, which is now in the American Museum of Natural History, is 64 feet long and could carry forty persons and their baggage. The men paddling are slaves from various tribes.

Chapter Eleven

Northwest Fishermen

THE VARIOUS TRIBES that lived along the rainy northwest coast have been called "capitalist" Indians. Blankets woven from the hair of dogs and mountain goats were their equivalent of one, or five, or ten, dollar bills. A rich man had thousands and thousands of blankets that he stored away in cedar chests—or loaned out at interest. Instead of gold and silver coins, he was likely to have strings of a rare seashell called dentalium. Instead of stocks and bonds, he prided himself on big plates of copper, each one worth possibly three, four, or even six thousand blankets in his money. A wealthy man might also invest in slaves, but his biggest investment was in names. He was a nobody unless he could boast at least one expensive name.

Among almost all Indian peoples, names were important. A boy might earn his name by having a special vision or by performing a feat of bravery. A man might acquire a new one by being elected to fill a post of honor. There was often magic power or religious significance attached to names. But the Northwest Indians went even further. They centered their lives around the right to use titles that were thought to bring great honor and prestige. They considered a man important not for what he did but for the names he had, and if he owned two—one for summer and one for winter—so much the better. Each family possessed a supply of hereditary titles that could be used by only one person at a time. A man made complicated and expensive deals which might cost him thousands of blankets in order to establish his right to assume a name belonging to his family or to his wife's.

The custom of using blankets and shells for money was only possible because the Northwest tribes had great wealth of another kind—they had an inexhaustible supply of food. Every spring salmon by the millions left the deep sea and swam up rivers looking for the fresh water in which they had been born and in which they would die after laying their eggs. In a few days or at most in a few weeks, fishermen caught enough food to last their families a whole year.

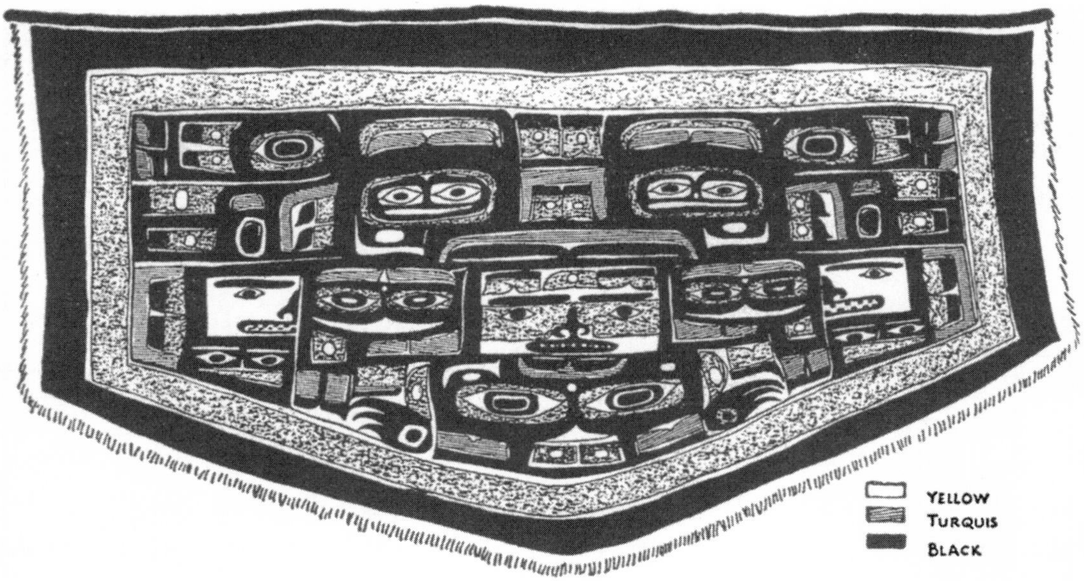

Designs for Northwest coast blankets like this one were stylized representations of people and animals.

Wealth of another kind—great red cedar trees—grew straight and tall in the rain-drenched forests that crowded down the mountainsides to the very beaches. From the cedars came houses, boats, dishes, baskets, tools, and even clothes. Salmon and cedar together made the fishing tribes the best-fed, best-housed Indians north of Mexico. Possibly they would also have been the best dressed if they had needed much clothing. But the climate was mild, so people wore nothing at all in the house and little or no clothes outdoors. They did dress up for special occasions, however, and one of these was a whale hunt.

The Tlinget Indians in Alaska gambled with ivory dice thrown on a leather tablet that looked like this.

The two points of this salmon harpoon are made of elk horn, and the line is made of elk sinew.

A rich man, wearing his best robe of sea otter or bearskin, would head out to sea standing in the bow of a huge canoe. Behind him eight men hired for the occasion paddled and steered. Beside him lay a harpoon with a detachable head—an invention borrowed from the Eskimos and one that the whalers of New England did not make until 1848. Before then the white man had attached the line to the wooden shaft of his spearlike harpoon and, since the shaft often broke, he had often lost his whale. The Indians attached their line to the harpoon head itself. When the head was firmly embedded in the flesh, the animal seldom escaped. The moment they struck a whale, the hunters began to pay out the line to which they tied floats made of inflated sealskins. The floats served as markers in the water, and they made it hard for the whale to dive and tired him out quickly.

With the help of other canoes in the expedition, the hunter towed his catch home. He beached it at high tide, and everyone in the village came to peel off thick layers of blubber. The whaler himself decided which part each assistant should get as pay. Then he decorated a chunk of blubber with duck feathers and maybe eagle feathers, too, and performed a ceremony to please the spirit of the whale. The ceremony was like a wake. People sat up for four days and nights, singing and dancing in honor of the huge animal that had done them the favor of visiting their village. Afterward they had a great feast. Everyone stuffed himself with blubber out of which the oil had been boiled.

A net used for dipping salmon out of the water once they had been caught.

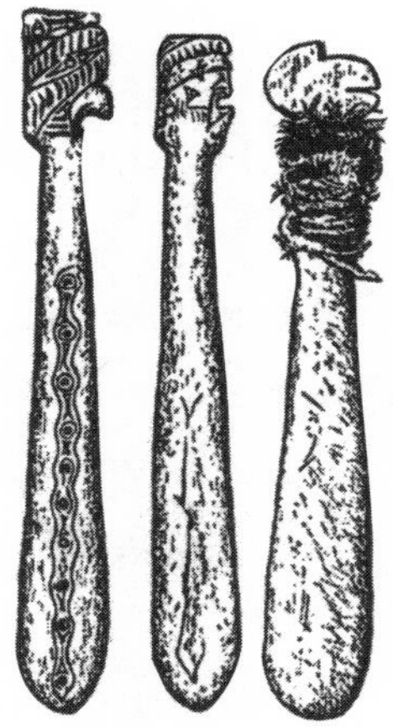

After landing a salmon a fisherman killed it with a club. Here are three different styles of salmon club.

Whale oil was a valuable product. It was used as a flavoring for smoked salmon or dried clams—even for berries. The fishermen dipped almost everything they ate into little bowls of oil before putting it into their mouths, and they wiped their fingers frequently on napkins of cedar bark which women or slaves stood ready to hand around. People of the fishing tribes always washed before and after a meal. Like all Indians who lived near water, they were very clean in their personal habits.

The great whaling canoes were exceedingly valuable. It often took two or three years to make one from a single huge red cedar tree. The Indian men cut the tree down by holding red-hot stones against the trunk with tongs made of wood that did not burn easily. Then they cut the charred part away with a stone axe. To guard against starting a forest fire, the men wrapped the tree trunk, above and below the cut, with wet seaweed or large wet leaves. Once the tree was felled, they floated it down to their village, which was always on a riverbank or by the seashore. There a carpenter went to work. He burned and chipped the log away, hollowing the inside and shaping the outside. As the hull of the canoe took shape, he drilled holes occasionally to measure its thickness, then carefully plugged them up again. When the burning and chipping were finished, he had a canoe that was no wider than the tree from which it came. To make it broader in the beam, he filled it with water into which he dropped hot rocks. This softened the wood so that he could force the sides outward and hold them apart with braces. Then he emptied the water and let the canoe dry in its new shape. Finally, using wooden pegs he added a high prow, and smoothed the outside with a sharkskin which was like sandpaper. Along the side of the boat were carved grotesque animals or birds, who supposedly invested the boat with their particular virtues of speed or strength.

The soft wood of the red cedar could be worked easily with tools of

A family totem appearing on a Northwestern plank house. A bird representing thunder has a whale in its talons. In the upper left is the lightning snake; in the upper right, a wolf. After white men brought metal axes, some Northwest Indians carved their totems on huge poles outside their homes.

A Northwest Coast wooden box. The sides and bottom are sewed together.

stone and bone. Using bone wedges, the carpenter split logs into boards—something no other North American Indians did. The long planks went into the building of great barnlike communal houses that stood in straight rows in villages that were always close to the water. In some tribes the boards of a house were sewed together and hung down a little like the slats of Venetian blinds. Although the houses were windowless they were well ventilated because of the cracks between the planks. This loose arrangement had another advantage. The inhabitants could lift up a board and thrust out a dead body. If they had had to carry it through the door, they would have felt they had to destroy the whole house in order to keep spirits from doing them harm.

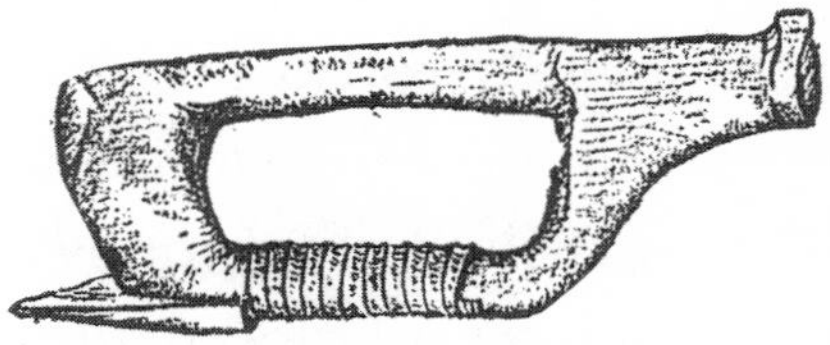

Carpenters shaped wood by pulling adzes over the wood toward themselves as carpenters do in the Orient. The adze at the left has a sharp blade made from a rock called jadeite.

So great was the sense of ownership among the Northwesterners that, although they lived in communal houses, each family owned the boards that made up the roof and outside walls of its own apartment. If a family moved out, it took its boards along. Sharing, which was so common among other Indian tribes, was almost unknown here, although Northwesterners did give things away on a grand scale.

The smaller structure to the left of the large plank building is a sweathouse. Indians in many parts of America built sweathouses where they took steam baths as part of their purification rites. They produced steam by pouring water on hot rocks.

A huge plank house like this accommodated many families. When the Indians came indoors on a rainy day, they took off all their clothes. After they adopted the white man's custom of wearing clothes all the time, however, many died of pneumonia from keeping on their wet clothes. (Based on a drawing in the Royal Ontario Museum.)

Like the Lakota, the Northwest Indians held giveaway feasts, known as a "potlatches," but they were given in a much different spirit from those of the Lakota. A potlatch began when a man decided to make a public announcement that he had the right to some very important name, like Always-Giving-Away-Blankets-While-Talking, Too-Rich, From-Whom-Presents-Are-Expected, or Throwing-Away-Property. To assemble his guests, among whom he always numbered his greatest rivals and enemies, he sent messengers by canoe, sometimes hundreds of miles.

Everyone who received an invitation knew he had to accept or be disgraced. Guests came with no spirit of celebration, for they had to eat everything that was put before them, no matter how uncomfortable it made them. They had to listen to long, insulting speeches from their host, who bragged insufferably about the greatness of his new name. Worst of all was the time after the feasting when the host began to give gifts. To his worst enemy he presented the biggest pile of blankets or perhaps one of the copper plates worth several thousand blankets. The recipient knew that he must give a potlatch of

A Northwest mother with a flattened forehead holds her baby whose head will be flattened from lying on the cradle board. The small diagram shows how these shaping boards work. (From a painting in the Royal Ontario Museum.)

his own and return a gift of much greater value than the one he had received. The host was really lending out blankets at interest, and custom required the guests to pay it no matter how exorbitant the cost. In the Kwakiutl tribe the rate of interest was one hundred percent a year. If a man did not repay, he was utterly disgraced, and it sometimes happened that he sold himself into slavery in order to discharge the debt.

Gifts were both a form of investment and a means of waging war. A rich leader in one village could get revenge on a leader in another by forcing him into bankruptcy. In addition, he might disgrace his enemy by showing how much property, in addition to the gifts, he could afford to destroy. He might throw a copper plate into the fire where it melted down and then dare any of his guests to do the same. He might tear up beautiful blankets, knock holes in the bottom of his best canoe, burn his house down, or even kill a slave or two. Guests who could not equal these feats of destruction went away in shame.

In every way the Northwesterners were obsessed with the idea of wealth. Those who were born into rich families spent a great deal of energy and imagination keeping their wealth, getting more, or showing off what they had. Below them in the social scale were those who thought of themselves as poor because they did not have the most desirable names or were not allowed to learn such lucrative crafts as whaling and carpentry. Actually there was so much food and material for other needs that the poor had about the same comforts as the wealthy. The only thing they lacked was prestige. It sometimes happened, however, that a poor boy was filled with such envy and ambition that he succeeded in accumulating a large pile of blankets and maybe even a copper plate during his lifetime.

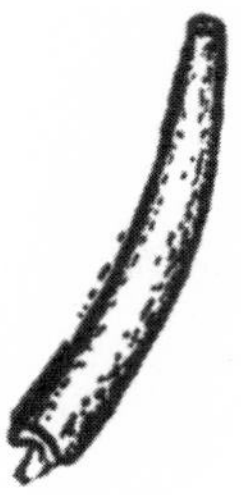

One of the rare dentalium shells that Northwest Indians used as a kind of money. They gathered dentalia by pushing a broomlike tool (top) down through the water and over the tip of the shell. A ring slid down over the broom's bristles and held them firmly around the shell as the fisherman gave an upward tug and pulled the dentalium loose.

At the bottom of the scale were the slaves, many of them captives or the children of captives taken during raids on other villages. While they lived comfortably and were treated almost as members of the family, they had a lifelong burden of disgrace to bear. Moreover, they could not escape the discouraging knowledge that they could never do anything to bring them honor or respect.

A man who wanted a wife from a noble family had to pay a high price for her, and he kept on paying her family every year if he expected her to remain in his house. He needed at least one wife, for it was she who wove his blankets.

Wool for the blankets came chiefly from little white dogs which the women kept isolated on islands. They also used the hair of mountain goats which they got in trade from Indians who lived inland. It was almost impossible for hunters to track down these shy creatures among the high peaks, but every spring the goats shed their hair, which could be gathered from the bushes on which it rubbed off. The inland tribes wanted salmon, whale oil, and dried clams, for which they exchanged tanned skins, jerked meat, other non-fish foods, and goat hair.

Often the people of many tribes met together at large fairs where they traded and gambled and had a general holiday. New ideas passed back and forth between the inland people and the seafaring people. The rich coastal tribes borrowed whatever they could make use of from every direction. As a result, their culture had in it something of the life of all the native peoples of western Canada, the northwestern United States, and Alaska.

It is possible that their culture had its roots even farther away. The Northwest Indians wore cone-shaped hats much like the headgear of the Chinese. The designs on their canoes and blankets were similar to those of some of the island dwellers of the Pacific. Many of them had mustaches and looked like the earliest inhabitants of the islands of Japan, rather than the smooth-faced Indians in the rest of the United States.

Northwestern rain capes and skirts were made from cedar bark. The Chinese-style hats were woven from spruce root.

One of their woodworking tools, the adze, appears nowhere else in North America, but it was commonly used in the Orient.

Actually, a way existed for boats from the Far East to reach the shores along which the coastal tribes lived. The warm Japanese current today often brings floating objects from Asia to Alaska, to Canada, and to the northwestern United States. Possibly at some time in the remote past Chinese junks were carried by the current across the Pacific. Certainly this happened at least once, for a Chinese coin was found among the prehistoric remains of one group of Northwest fishermen. Whether the junk also brought sailors, nobody knows, but the well-fed, energetic Indians along the coast got an amazing variety of ideas and customs from someplace, and with them they built up a bizarre life unlike any other in America.

Chapter Twelve

Arctic Inventors

Of all the peoples we call Indians, the last to reach this continent were the Eskimos. They paddled across the Bering Strait in little skin boats, perhaps three thousand years ago, and settled along the six thousand miles of inhospitable Arctic coast that stretches from eastern Siberia to eastern Greenland. Two remarkable devices made it possible for them to live in the treeless waste that was covered with snow and ice for much of each year. One was the detachable or toggle harpoon. The other was the oil lamp, and neither invention would have done the trick without the other.

With the harpoon an Eskimo hunter could kill and recover seal, walrus, and even whales—something that was impossible with a spear or bow and arrow. The body of a dead sea mammal merely sank out of sight beneath the water and was lost unless the barb that killed it was tied to a line. Sea animals provided not only food, clothing, tents, and bone for tools but also a fine oil that meant the difference between life and death for human beings in the intense Arctic cold. The oil burned with a white, almost smokeless flame that gave light and heat to Eskimo dwellings when it was used in a bowl-like stone lamp with a wick made of dried moss.

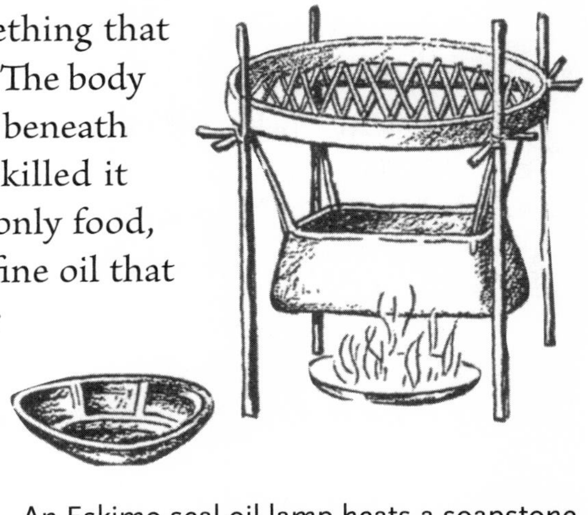

An Eskimo seal oil lamp heats a soapstone pot hung over it. Above the pot is a rack on which wet clothes are dried.

An Eskimo was never far from his lamp, and his lamp was never far from the sea, for no land animal produced an oil thin enough to soak up into the wick. The inventions that gave him freedom to live in the Arctic also tied him to a narrow strip of barren coastland. Scattered in small family groups, Eskimos were independent individualists. Every man considered himself the equal of every other. He was far too busy getting food for his family to engage in fighting as a sport in the fashion of the Sioux or Iroquois, and he had no time for elaborate ceremonies like those of the Pueblo Indians.

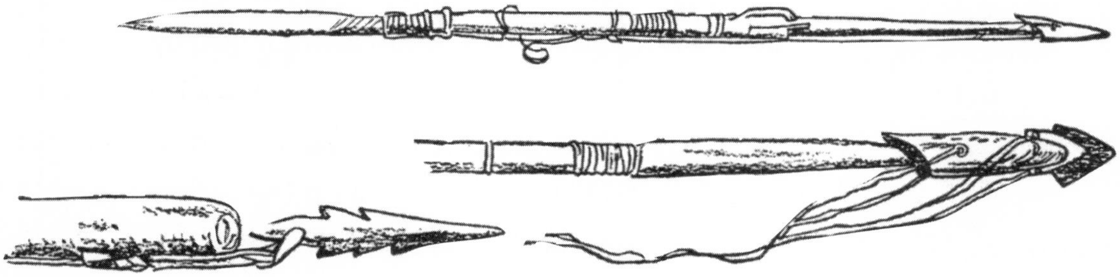

Various harpoons and harpoon heads. Note that the head can come loose from the shaft and is tied to a sinew line.

Still, many a settlement did have an "angakok"—a sort of combination medicine man and magician: a shaman. One of the angakok's jobs was to find out what caused illness and to prescribe cures. He believed that people got sick when they broke sacred rules. If, for example, a man ate both caribou meat and seal meat on the same day, it might give him anything from a toothache to an infected toe. The angakok might advise the patient to avoid doing any work on deerskin for a certain length of time. Or he might tell the whole village not to wash for several days. Often when he made his diagnosis, he actually fell into a trance and thought he took trips to the moon or to the underground homes of spirits who ruled the world. At other times he simply put on a good show. He used ventriloquism to give a realistic effect when he was talking to spirits, and to make his special powers all the more convincing he escaped like Houdini from knotted ropes.

Even though an Eskimo believed in spirits, he also had faith in practical tools, and he solved most of his problems by

One style of kayak, the light skin-covered boats in which Eskimos fished and hunted. Out in a kayak they wore waterproof garments made of seal or walrus intestines.

Left: An Eskimo drills holes in walrus ivory, bone, and bits of driftwood. Holding the upper end of the drill in his mouth, he whirls it with a back-and-forth motion of the bow, whose string is wrapped around the drill. Right: a drill and bow.

making ingenious inventions and doing endless skilled work with his hands. Using only the few materials that were available, Eskimos created extraordinary implements and devices. They put sleds together from small pieces of scarce driftwood, bone, and sinew and built up runners out of ice. They trained dogs to pull the sleds and thus developed better means of transportation than any other Indians had before the arrival of Europeans. Their unsinkable little kayaks made it possible for them to fish safely in icy waters far from shore. Eskimo clothing, too, was most expertly made. Women, using ivory needles, could sew absolutely waterproof seams in sealskin and deerskin. This was of greatest importance in the North, where a leaky pair of boots might mean frozen feet.

Some Eskimo groups were adept at building three different kinds of house, or igloo: a pit house made of stone, driftwood, and whalebone covered with earth for permanent quarters; a snow house for use while hunting seals out on the Arctic ice; and a portable skin tent for caribou-hunting trips in summer.

The Eskimos were first-rate mechanics. They used flexible whalebone to make elaborate snares for birds. With the same material they fashioned a trap that killed polar bears by going off inside the animals. The

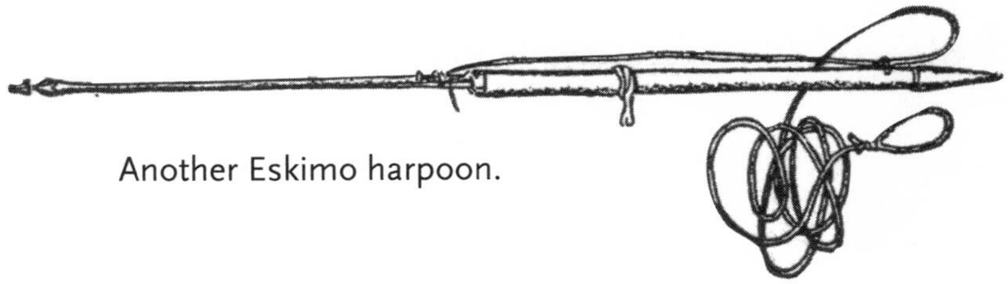

Another Eskimo harpoon.

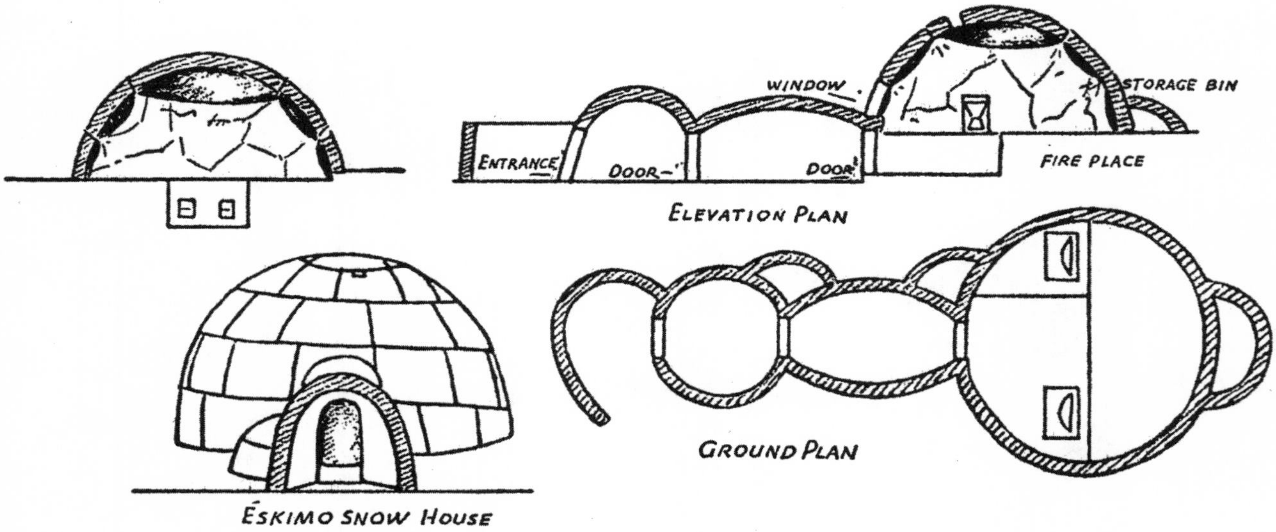

Diagrams of a snow igloo. Dogs were sheltered in the long, low entrance tunnel which led to the house. People slept without clothes between furs on the snow ledge opposite the entrance. Storage bins held frozen fish and meat. An inner lining of skin provided a dead air space for insulation. Sometimes a window was made of clear ice.

bear first ate a chunk of bait made by coiling a piece of whalebone up like a spring inside a ball of fat. When the fat melted in the bear's stomach, the bone straightened out and tore at his vitals.

Deft fingers created all kinds of games that men, women, and children played between naps in the long Arctic night. Families played together in solitary igloos when they went off on winter sealing expeditions, or they competed in groups if they lived in settlements on the shore. When group celebrations were possible, the Eskimos joined in them with gusto. There was literally no people in the world who took a greater joy in living. Laughter and inventions were their courageous answer to the bleak world around them.

The Eskimos' tough, quarrelsome dogs could pull heavy sleds great distances.

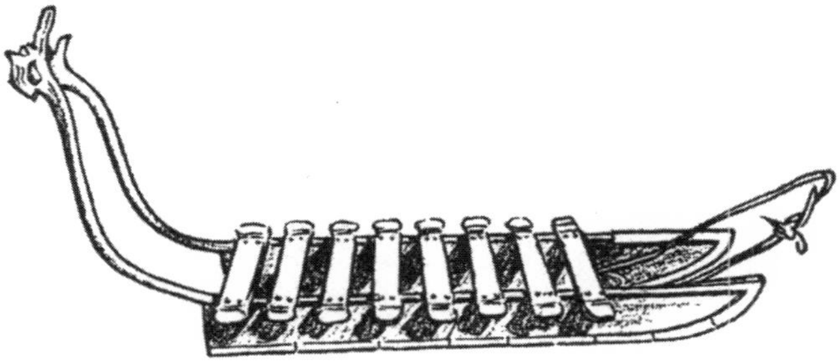

A sled made of bits of driftwood and bone with caribou horns for steering handles.

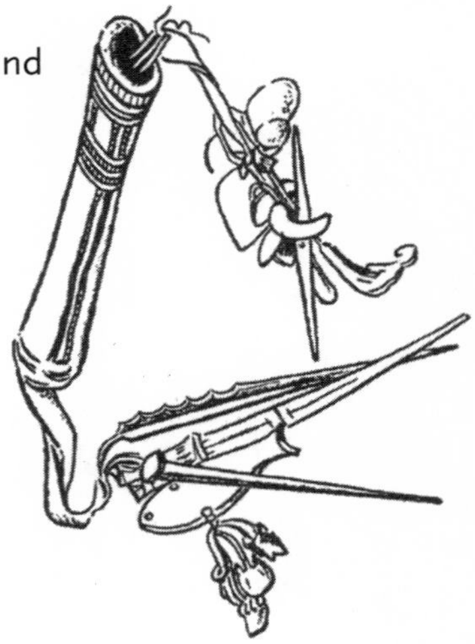

Bone needles and needle case.

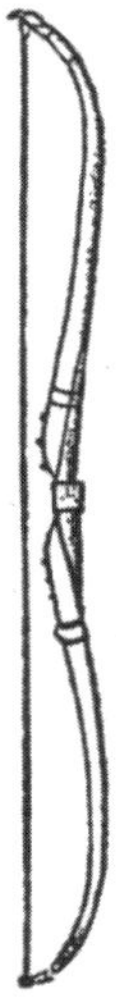

Bow made from separate pieces of wood bound and strengthened with sinew.

Thimble made of sealskin.

Knife with bone handle.

Left to right: Eastern and Western Eskimo dolls.

Hudson Bay Eskimo fishhook and line.

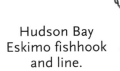

Alaskan Eskimo stone sinker used in fishing with a tine.

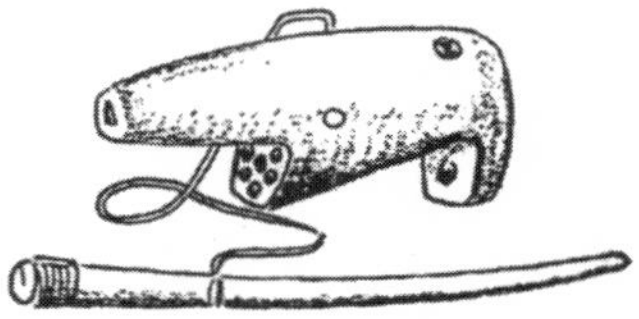

Equipment for a game, in which a player throws the larger ivory piece into the air and then tries to spear it by thrusting the thin ivory stick through one of the holes.

Ivory box for small objects.

Hook used for pulling big fish out of the water.

Arrow with a bone point.

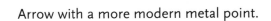

Arrow with a more modern metal point.

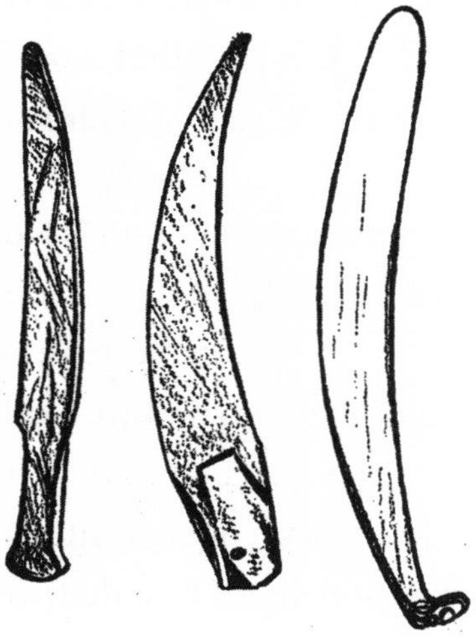

Three knives used for cutting blocks of snow to build houses.

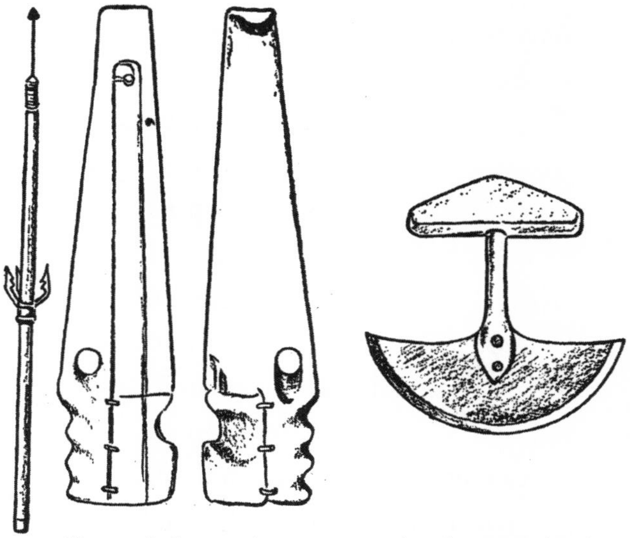

Above, left to right: Dart used in hunting birds. A throwing board for launching the dart: this elaboration of the ancient spear-thrower gave the hunter extra power; the dart lay in the groove which ran almost the length of the board. The reverse side of the throwing board: the notches at the bottom fitted the thumb and three fingers; the hole was for the index finger; this arrangement gave the hunter very accurate control. An "ulo" or woman's knife used in cutting skins.

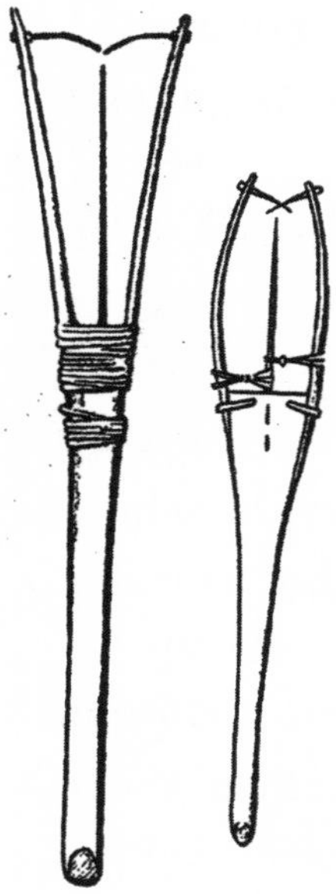

Two kinds of fish spear.

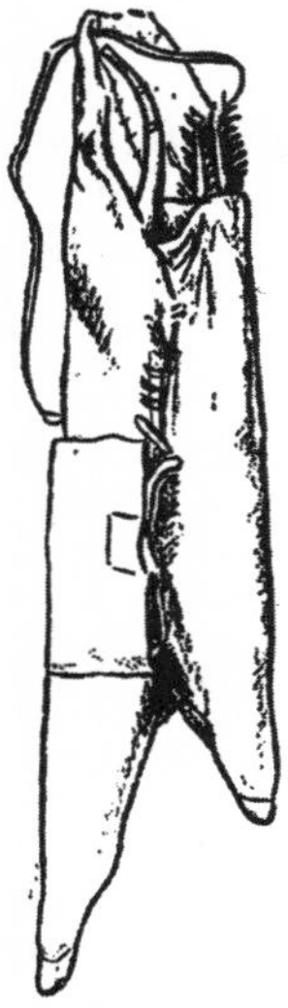

An Eskimo quiver with separate compartments for bow and arrows.

Ivory figurines of a fox and geese, used in a game.

Float used in whale hunting, made of a whole sealskin blown up with air.

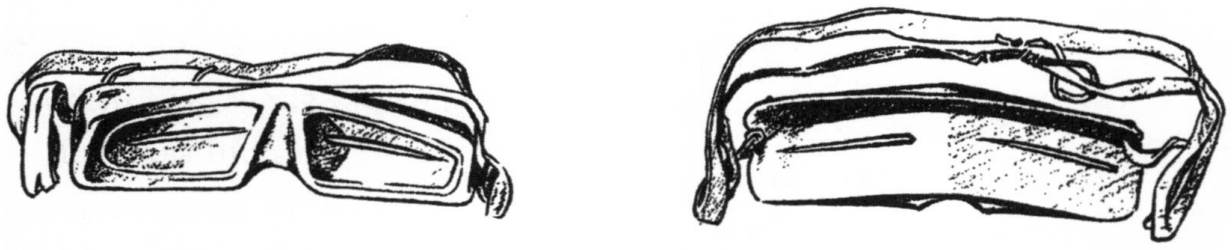

To prevent snow blindness caused by reflection of sunlight, Eskimos carved goggles from ivory with only tiny slits through which to peer. Left: how goggles fitted over the nose. Right: front view of goggles.

Chapter Thirteen

The Largest Tribe—The Navahos

NAVAHO SAY THAT a member of their tribe who is a shortwave radio fan had a strange experience recently. He was talking in English to another ham in Alaska who, as it happened, was also an Indian, a member of an Athapascan tribe. Just for the fun of it, each said a few words in his own Indian tongue. To their amazement and delight, they could understand each other. The two languages were not exactly the same, but there was no doubt that the Navaho could speak more easily to the Athapascan radio operator in Alaska than he could to his Hopi, Zuni, or Ute neighbors in New Mexico and Arizona.

Behind this lies a story—several stories, in fact. More than a thousand years ago a sprawling tribe of primitive hunters who spoke the Athapascan language lived just south of Eskimo country in Alaska and northwestern Canada. Like the Eskimos, the Athapascans were late arrivals from Siberia, and like the Eskimos they brought with them bows that were reinforced and made powerful with sinews. Many Athapascan groups settled down in the forests near the Arctic. But others moved southward.

Some traveled along the California coast. Others struck inland and passed through the Paiute country in Nevada. Still others may have followed the Rocky Mountains. After taking various routes at different times, many of

Woman weaving one of the famous Navaho blankets, which they usually sell to traders or tourists. Navahos learned the art of weaving from the neighboring Pueblos, where men customarily practiced this craft.

these people finally got together again in the Southwest. Here their powerful Asiatic bows proved of decisive importance. With them the Athapascans were able to turn into successful raiders. The Pueblos called these newcomers Apaches, meaning "enemies." When some of the "enemies" learned how to grow corn for themselves, they were known as "Apaches de navahu," or "enemies who have the cultivated fields." The name soon became simply "Navaho," and it has been that ever since. The name "Apache" also persisted. Gradually the Navahos and Apaches divided into separate tribes, living in different ways and speaking different dialects of the same language. The Navahos were quick at learning new ways as they raided first their Pueblo neighbors and later the Spaniards. They stole horses and became expert riders. They ran off flocks of sheep and learned how to tend them. Now they had plenty of meat and wool which captive Pueblos taught them to weave into blankets.

Corn and mutton meant that more Navaho babies grew to manhood, and the tribe increased rapidly. Using their captured horses, they made more and more raids against their neighbors, particularly the Spanish who had the largest flocks of sheep. Between 1846 and 1850, they stole from one district alone

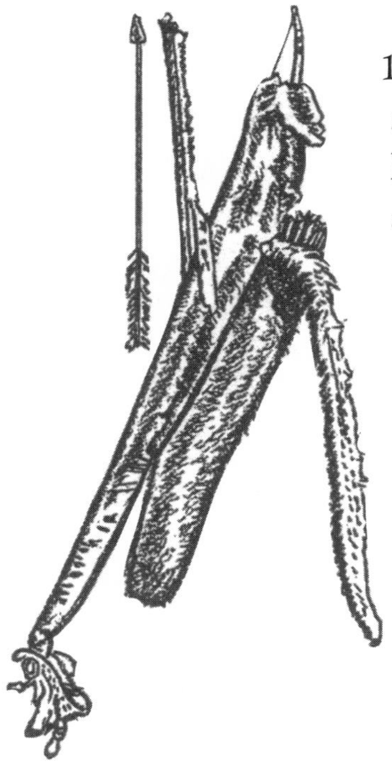

An old Navaho quiver, which is very similar to the Eskimo type on page 130. The Athapascan ancestors of the Navahos were neighbors of the Eskimos.

12,000 mules, 7,000 horses, 31,000 cattle, and 450,000 sheep. They were a vigorous, fearless people who took livestock from other Indians and from whites as eagerly as the whites took land from the Indians and from each other. It was a mark of honor and not a crime among the Navahos to steal from your enemies.

During the Civil War their raids were such a great nuisance to the Northern side that the Government sent Kit Carson with seven hundred volunteers to round up the Navahos and put them on a reservation where they were supposed to take up a peaceful life as farmers. Carson, an experienced old trapper and scout, knew he could not find the men all together at one time and defeat them in battle. "The People," as they called themselves, tended their flocks over a huge area. They had two mountain ranges in which to hide, and deep canyons with sides so steep that there was no way into them except at either end. Professional soldiers had failed again and again to round up the elusive herdsmen and their families. Carson resolved not to repeat their errors but to try a method he was sure would work—and one that would prevent a great deal of bloodshed, too. He starved the Navahos into submission by destroying all their cornfields and killing every sheep he could find. One by one the Navahos surrendered at Army Headquarters in Fort Defiance in order to get the food that was promised to them there.

Then, in 1864, came the saddest year in Navaho history—the event from which modern Navaho history begins. The once proud and independent shepherds and horsemen had to walk meekly day after weary day as the Army herded them three hundred miles eastward from Arizona to a small reservation in New Mexico. There nothing went right. The crops failed. People sickened and died. But the Navahos learned a shocking fact that they had never dreamed of in their isolation. The

Navahos learned the art of making silver jewelry from the Spanish. Here are a silver buckle and a necklace with "squash blossom" pendants.

might of the white man was much greater than their own. Never again could they take up their old life as the feared masters of the Southwest.

In 1868 they signed a treaty that allowed them to return to their old homes between the beautiful ragged Chuska Mountains and the great flat-topped Black Mountain in Arizona. With new sheep the Government gave them, the Navahos started life all over again. And there they live today—the largest Indian tribe in the country and the most rapidly growing group in the entire population of the United States.

Several times the reservation has been enlarged to take care of the increasing number of people and their wide-wandering flocks. The jagged red cliffs, the forest-covered mountaintops, and sagebrush desert of Navaholand make up an area as large as New Hampshire, Vermont, Connecticut, and Rhode Island. But even this huge territory is too small. Seventy-five thousand Navahos are supposed to live as shepherds on arid land that cannot support half that many, and it is quite literally true that the harder they try the less they succeed. Their sheep overgraze and kill the grass. When the grass goes, the soil underneath it goes, and this means an ever-decreasing area for grazing. Plainly the Navahos must find new ways of making a living. This is not easy, because eighty percent of them are illiterate and fifty percent cannot even speak English.

Although their treaty with the United States government provided one schoolroom for each thirty children, the treaty has never been kept, and only half of the Navaho youngsters get the beginnings of a grade school education. Every meeting of the Navaho Tribal Council today is one long plea for the Government to build and staff more schools and for the Navahos to take advantage of them. Without education they are doomed to continuing poverty and disease. The infant mortality and tuberculosis rates are higher on the Navaho reservation than anywhere else in the country.

To gain courage for facing all these great difficulties, the Navahos cling to their old customs, to their religion, and to their language. Medicine men called Singers conduct long and beautiful ceremonies to cure the strange new diseases that white men have brought. In high-pitched voices that soar up to falsetto they sing songs connected with old legends. These songs, if done properly, please the spirits that can drive away illness. So do dances performed in the right costumes and with the right figures and rhythms. The Singer makes sand paintings, too. On the floor of a sick person's "hogan," or one-room house of logs and mud, he sprinkles different-colored sands and with amazing precision builds up pictures which grow out of Navaho legends and are an important part of many curing ceremonies.

Side by side with the ceremonies, which sometimes last for nine days and involve hundreds of people who come to help the patient with their presence and their prayers, are modern hospitals, doctors, and nurses. The Singer and the Field Nurse from the Indian Service may both attend a patient at the same time. Singers, sprinkling sacred pollen on the walls, blessed a new hospital at Fort Defiance.

Everywhere in Navaholand the new rubs shoulders with the old. The people still keep many horses. Like typical western cowboys, the men usually dress in blue jeans and wear Stetson hats. But along with horses and wagons there are hundreds of pickup trucks bumping over the rutted roads of the reservation. Men who a hundred years ago would have been tinkering with their strong sinew-backed bows are now tinkering with carburetors. People who until quite recently chopped down trees with fire and stone axes now run a sawmill owned by the Navaho Tribe, and some of them shape wood into fine furniture in a tribe-owned factory.

Typical hogans are six-sided, roofed over with earth, and windowless. Every hogan faces east.

The younger men have turned from rainmaking ceremonies to building water-conservation dams and irrigation ditches. Now and then a Navaho pilot flies his plane to a distant hogan and takes a patient away to a hospital. Navaho miners are beginning to tap the reservation's great coal beds. Helium gas, gas for cooking and heating, and the miraculous new source of power—uranium—all lie beneath the soil of the reservation. But the Navaho who spends his day drilling for oil or blasting uranium-bearing ore out of his sacred Chuska Mountains still goes home at night to a one-room hogan where the most modern conveniences are a wood-burning stove and a kerosene lamp. He drinks water from a barrel that has been hauled many miles from the nearest spring. He greets his baby who is still tied to a cradle board as babies in the Southwest have been tied for thousands of years.

Navahos are beginning to bridge the gap between life as shepherds and life in the world of industry and science. They are a vigorous new nation developing within the larger American nation. While using all that seems practical to them from white culture, they still proudly keep their identity as Navahos. The airplane pilot or the truck driver or the short-wave radio fan is as surely Navaho as he is a modern man.

Hopis, who still perform their Snake Dance every year, live on a reservation entirely surrounded by the larger Navaho reservation.

Chapter Fourteen

Famous Indians

AMERICA BEGAN TO be overcrowded the day that white colonists first arrived. Fewer than a million Indians lived in the territory that is now the United States, but there was not room enough for them with their old way of life and for the energetic Europeans as well. The hunting tribes needed an enormous area in which to search for game, and primitive farmers with only stone implements needed many more acres from which to choose their fields than European farmers with their modern wagons, axes, horses, and plows.

At first the Indians willingly let the English, French, and Spanish move onto their lands, but very soon they found their own way of life being threatened. As one Lenape chief put it, "The English claim all on one side of the river and the French claim all on the other. Where is the land of the Indians?"

Most Europeans, who knew that they had better weapons, tools, and knowledge, believed also that they were designed by nature to be a superior people with superior rights. They felt justified in taking whatever they wanted, and they did so, using means both fair and unfair. Soon the Indians were struggling to survive.

From the very first they met their problems in two ways. A few individuals, quickly recognizing the white man's superior strength, tried to make alliances with the Europeans who offered them the most trade and other advantages. Most Indians, however, had no opportunity to work out a peaceful adjustment to the new life that was flooding around them. They reacted like any self-respecting courageous people. They fought for their land. For nearly three hundred years they kept up a stubborn war of defense. "These lands are ours," Tecumseh said to General Harrison. "No one has a right to remove us, because we were the first owners. As to boundaries, the Great Spirit above knows no boundaries, nor will his red children acknowledge any. . . . You and I will have to fight it out."

Out of the struggle leaders arose among the Indians, some of them very great indeed. Many were brilliant military planners. Others were statesmen, quite as able as any of the Europeans with whom they dealt. Still others distinguished themselves as peacemakers or as individuals, like Sequoyah, who saw a future for his people if they learned to take full advantage of the white man's knowledge.

Here are some of the great Indians of the past, arranged roughly in the order in which they appeared on the stage of history.

Pocahontas, a Powhatan of Virginia (1595–1617). The early English explorer Captain John Smith was something of a braggart and bully, and he expected the Indians he met in Virginia to do as he ordered. The Powhatans endured his arrogance for a while, but finally, so legend has it, they captured him. As they were about to execute him for what they considered his crimes against them, Pocahontas, the daughter of Powhatan, the chief of the Powhatan tribes, saved his life.

Whether she actually did so is doubtful, but it is a fact that the English later kidnapped her and held her as hostage. While in captivity she met the Englishman John Rolfe whom she later married. Rolfe took her to England where people called her a princess and treated her as one. After giving birth to a son, Thomas, Pocahontas

Pocahontas

died of smallpox. Thomas Rolfe eventually went to Virginia and from him members of the famous Randolph family claimed descent.

Squanto, a Wampanoag of Massachusetts (?–1622). Fourteen years before the Pilgrims landed in Massachusetts, a British vessel dropped anchor in Plymouth harbor. The crew took aboard a cargo of fish and beaver skins they got from the Wampanoag Indians who lived there in the village of Patuxet. At the last moment the Englishmen also seized some of the Indians themselves to sell as slaves. Among these was a young boy named Squanto. After growing up in London as a household slave, Squanto returned to his old home a few months before the Pilgrims arrived. There he found his village deserted. The entire population had been wiped out by some epidemic, possibly brought by the white traders.

Fortunately for the Pilgrims he remained nearby and promptly took up residence with them, acting as interpreter and teacher. He showed the Pilgrims how to plant the corn they pilfered from the Wampanoags. He taught them to cultivate and to fertilize the soil with dead fish. In many ways Squanto, who understood both Indian and English life, made it possible for the first New England settlement to survive.

King Philip, a Wampanoag sachem of Massachusetts (?–1676). From the day the Pilgrims settled at Plymouth the Wampanoags sought to live at peace with their new neighbors. Under the leadership of their hereditary sachem Massassoit they never waged war. His son Metacom, whom the English called King Philip, also kept the peace for many years. But the Pilgrims and Puritans moved farther and farther into the Indians' land, until the Wampanoag hunting grounds were nearly gone. In addition, the settlers tried to make the Wampanoags obey laws laid down by the English king.

King Philip decided that the only way to save his people and their land was to drive out the English. An able leader and organizer, he built a confederation of New England tribes, and in 1675 he launched a war against the white settlements. His warriors destroyed twelve towns, damaged forty more, and killed hundreds of colonists.

In spite of King Philip's resourcefulness and courage, the English were so numerous and their weapons so powerful that in the end the Wampanoags were completely wiped out as a tribe. Many were sold into slavery in the West Indies, among them King Philip's wife and small son. All that remained to remind the people that there had once been a King Philip was his head which the colonists had severed from his body when he fell in battle and which was displayed in Plymouth for twenty years.

Pope, a Tewa of the San Juan Pueblo in New Mexico (?–c. 1690). The year that King Philip launched his war in Massachusetts, a medicine man named Pope sat in a little adobe jail in New Mexico. He was accused of practicing witchcraft, because he conducted the ceremonies of his ancient religion. Also he was accused, with others, of murdering Spanish priests. Quite probably he was guilty of both charges.

The mood of the Pueblos was grim and bitter. They were angry at being forced to worship a strange foreign god, and they wanted to return to their own rituals, which they thought brought rain and which certainly gave them comfort in their time of suffering. They were ready for any desperate action in order to be free from the harsh Spaniards who had virtually turned them into slaves.

Somehow Pope escaped from jail and avoided the almost certain death penalty that awaited him. For five years he made intensive secret preparations for a revolt. Traveling long distances and talking with great persuasiveness, he bound the men of almost all the Pueblos together in a confederacy with a common plan. Then a traitor betrayed the date of the uprising.

As soon as he learned of the betrayal, Pope sent runners to all the Pueblos carrying knotted strings that gave the signal for the revolt to begin ahead of schedule. On August 10, 1680, the peaceful Pueblos took their bows, clubs, and stone knives and attacked the Spaniards who had guns, armor, and swords. Four hundred Spaniards including eighty-one priests fell before Pope's well-organized men, and the rest fled. For twelve years the Pueblos were free, but after Pope's death the confederacy weakened. The Spaniards returned and stayed on until they in turn were conquered by the United States Army more than one hundred and fifty years later.

Tammany, a Delaware chief of Pennsylvania (latter part of 17th century). Tammany, whose name meant "the affable one," was famed among both the Indians and whites as a wise, just, and generous chief. In 1683 he signed a treaty with William Penn, giving land in Pennsylvania to the Quakers, and during his lifetime the Delawares and the white men lived at peace.

Legends of Tammany's goodness grew up, and many of the colonists came to regard him as a saint. During the American Revolution hundreds of patriots joined St. Tammany societies which were strongly anti-British. One of these, still using such Indian words as wigwam and sachem, survives to this day in New York where it is a powerful political organization in the Democratic Party.

Pontiac

Pontiac, an Ottawa chief, Great Lakes region (c. 1720–69). After the British defeated the French and took control of Canada in 1760, Pontiac, the chief of the Ottawas, watched curiously to see what the Englishmen would do.

The French, with whom he was familiar, had come as traders, not settlers, but it was soon apparent that the British intended to occupy his tribe's lands. He then moved energetically to unite all the border tribes, even those who had long warred among themselves.

By the winter of 1763, this tall, brawny man had built a powerful confederacy and laid out a plan of war so effective that it shook the British Empire and brought in a new Prime Minister to lead the fight against him. To each tribe Pontiac assigned the task of attacking the fort nearest to it. At the end of May, all the tribes moved at the same time, and fort after fort fell. The Indians annihilated the garrisons and many of the surrounding settlements. Only two forts, the most important, did not immediately go down before the furious onslaught. One was on the present site of Pittsburgh and the other at Detroit.

Pontiac, leading the Ottawas and Ojibways in person, had a clever scheme for capturing Detroit which was very well fortified. He planned to take a large number of unarmed warriors into the fort for a peace conference. On the second day of the talks he and his men would conceal arms under their blankets and robes. At a signal the warriors would fall upon the soldiers. The plan was foolproof—except for one thing. A traitor, counting on favors from the British, gave the plan away.

The British locked themselves inside the heavy log palisade surrounding the fort, and Pontiac had no choice but to besiege the stronghold. Siege warfare was unknown to Indians who were accustomed only to quick attacks. But Pontiac was such a dynamic leader that he held the restless warriors together for six whole months—a feat unequaled by any Indian leader in all history. Pontiac and his men tried to keep help from reaching the beleaguered fort either overland or by water. But English reinforcements proved too great and Pontiac had to withdraw.

Later he tried to form another confederacy farther west, but an Illinois Indian was bribed with a barrel of rum to murder him. So great was Pontiac's prestige among the Ottawas that they immediately began a furious campaign of revenge against the Illinois, who in the end were all but wiped out.

Joseph Brant, a Mohawk chief of New York (1742–1807). When the American Revolution broke out, a great debate took place among the tribes in the Iroquois League. The British promised to help the Iroquois defend their lands against the colonists and they offered pay for American scalps. The American colonists merely requested that the Iroquois remain neutral. The debate ended in a split, with four of the tribes aiding the British, and two—the Oneidas and the Tuscaroras—taking no part in the war at all.

The leader of the pro-British Iroquois was Thayendanega (The One Who Holds Two Bets), a Mohawk chief known to the colonists as Joseph Brant. Brant was one of the few among his people who had received both an English education and full training as a warrior. He went to school in Connecticut and then became an interpreter. Later he fought on the side of the English against Pontiac and rose rapidly to the position of a war chief. In addition to this honor from his own people, special favors came to him from the English because his sister was the wife of Sir William Johnson, the chief British agent among the Iroquois. In 1775 he made a long visit in England, where he was much impressed with the wealth and power of the center of the British Empire. When he returned to America he was made an officer in the British army and during the Revolution he led the Iroquois war parties that spread terror among the American settlers in the Mohawk Valley.

Joseph Brant

After the British were defeated, he led the remnants of his tribe to Canada where they received land and settled down. In his last years Brant, a convert to Christianity, devoted much of his time to translating religious works into the Mohawk tongue, which missionaries had found a way of transcribing into the English alphabet.

Red Jacket, a Seneca chief of New York (c. 1756–1830). While Brant was rising as a military leader, a younger warrior who served under him was getting a reputation as a coward. Known as Red Jacket because he had once been given a red army coat by a British officer, this man clearly had little heart for warfare, and he won Brant's everlasting scorn by leaving the scene of a battle. In spite of the importance the Iroquois attached to physical bravery, Red Jacket became a chief and a powerful leader because he was an orator and could fight with words. Time after time he gave brilliant expression to his people's desire to keep both their lands and their identity as Indians.

Red Jacket

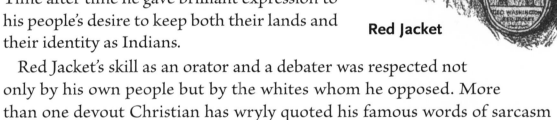

Red Jacket's skill as an orator and a debater was respected not only by his own people but by the whites whom he opposed. More than one devout Christian has wryly quoted his famous words of sarcasm about missionaries:

> [They] do us no good. . . . If they are not useful to white people, why do they send them among the Indians; if they are useful to the white people, and do them good, why do they not keep them at home? They [the white people] are surely bad enough to need the labor of every one who can make them better.

As Red Jacket grew older he grew increasingly bitter about the lot of the Iroquois. But up to the very end he cherished one thing he had received from the white men—a large medal President George Washington had personally given him at a conference held for the purpose of working out better relations between the Iroquois and the new American republic.

Alexander McGillivray, a Creek chief of Georgia and Alabama (c. 1738–1793). Although he was only one-quarter Indian and the heir to a comfortable fortune left him by his Scottish grandfather, McGillivray became the most influential member of the Creek tribe at the time of the American Revolution and afterward. As a colonel in the British army, he led ten thousand Creeks against the Colonial forces in the South. There he daringly played one group of white men against another for his own benefit and for the good of his tribe.

McGillivray was a master at conniving, and there was nothing small-scale about his schemes. He signed a secret treaty of friendship with President Washington with whom he had recently been at war. The terms of the agreement made him a brigadier general in the American army at a large salary. Then he promptly made a similar treaty with the Spanish rivals of the United States who controlled Florida, providing a salary more than double what Washington offered him. He collected from both. Somehow he managed to avoid being caught by the Americans in a Spanish uniform, and the Spanish never saw him dressed as an American general. As for the Creeks, they rejoiced in a leader who could hoodwink the whites. For once it was an Indian and not a European who played the old game of divide and conquer.

Sacajawea, a Shoshoni woman of the northern Rockies (c. 1787–?). Early explorers were often dependent on Indian guides to make their way through the wilderness. When Lewis and Clark crossed the continent to the northwest coast in 1804–1805, the actual guide and savior of the expedition was Sacajawea, the slave wife of a Frenchman hired to lead the party. Though she was only eighteen or nineteen and carried a baby all the way in a cradle board, Sacajawea led the explorers unharmed through the territories of many different tribes, across the forbidding Rocky Mountains, and back again. Her calmness, heroism, and ingenuity won the respect and affection of both Lewis and Clark, and Clark showed his gratitude by giving her son an education.

Accounts differ regarding Sacajawea's later life, but one that has much to support it says that she escaped from her worthless husband, lived for a while among the Comanches who were closely related to the Shoshonis, and finally rejoined her own people among whom she lived to be nearly a hundred. A wise old woman claiming to be Sacajawea was a trusted friend and adviser of the Shoshoni chief Washakie until her death in 1884.

Tecumseh, a Shawnee chief of the Ohio region (1768–1813). The westward advance of American settlers filled the young Shawnee chief Tecumseh with alarm. Like Pontiac before him he set about creating an alliance of tribes along the frontier. But Tecumseh's vision was greater than Pontiac's. He looked forward to a powerful Indian state, strong enough to live in peace and equality with the whites who would be forced to remain farther east.

Tecumseh

In his venture Tecumseh was supported by the British who still hoped to reclaim the colonies they had lost and were eager to use the grievances of the Indians to their own advantage. Traveling tirelessly along the frontier from Wisconsin to the Gulf of Mexico, Tecumseh visited tribe after tribe and spoke brilliantly of his dream of a war to end wars between Indians and white men—and between Indians themselves.

But Tecumseh's brother, a medicine man known as "the Prophet," disobeyed his instructions and launched a battle against American soldiers at Tippecanoe, Indiana, before Tecumseh was ready. General Harrison, who later became President of the United States, won such a tremendous victory that Tecumseh's federation of tribes fell apart.

When the War of 1812 broke out, Tecumseh sided with the British in the forlorn hope that by doing so he was aiding his people. In 1813 he fell in battle at the head of his warriors.

Petalesharo, a Pawnee chief, of Kansas and Nebraska (c. 1797–1841). For centuries the Pawnees engaged in a gruesome religious rite inherited from the Mound Builders. When in great trouble they sought to please their most powerful god, the Great Star (Saturn), by sacrificing a beautiful young woman captured from another tribe.

In 1817, as medicine men were preparing to burn a Comanche girl alive, a young chief, Petalesharo, defied the age-old religious customs of his people and prevented the sacrifice. Before the eyes of four hundred warriors he cut the bonds that held her to a stake, dashed off with her on horseback, then gave her food and a horse, and sent her back to her people.

Normally any Pawnee who committed such sacrilege would have been killed. But Petalesharo was known as the bravest and most skillful warrior in the tribe. No one dared touch him. Later, when the priests continued their custom in secret, he again freed the victims. By the time he died, the Pawnees had given up the practice of human sacrifice.

Osceola, a Seminole chief of Florida (c. 1803–1838). In the 1830s the United States government decided to remove all eastern Indian tribes to lands west of the Mississippi. At that time, a large group of Creeks known as Seminoles (meaning "runaways"), together with escaped African slaves who lived among them, fought a bitter war for their right to remain in Florida. The able leader in this war—which cost the United States the lives of fifteen hundred soldiers and $20,000,000—was a tall, slender young man named Osceola. First, he hid the Seminole women and children deep in a swamp. Then he ambushed any soldiers who ventured into his stronghold. When at last he agreed to attend a conference under a flag of truce, General Jessup of the US Army seized him and threw him into prison. There the brilliant young leader sickened and died. Most of the Seminoles were finally removed to what is now Oklahoma, but some who avoided capture are the ancestors of the Seminoles who live in Florida today.

Osceola

Ely S. Parker, a Seneca sachem of New York State (1828–1905). In 1861 an unsuccessful clerk in a small leather shop in Galena, Illinois, made friends with an educated Seneca sachem who was working as an engineer on a government building. The clerk was Ulysses S. Grant, and the Seneca was Ely S. Parker. Three years later, Grant had been made Commander in Chief of the Union forces in the Civil War, and Parker was his secretary. By the end of the war, Parker himself had risen to the rank of brigadier general, and the terms of surrender that General Lee signed at Appomattox were in Parker's handwriting.

When Grant became President, he appointed his Seneca friend Commissioner of Indian Affairs—the first and only Indian to hold that post.

Sitting Bull, a Lakota chief (1835–90). The most famous Lakota chief was deliberate and thoughtful when he was a boy. But at the age of fourteen he showed he could move swiftly enough, once he had decided to act. He entered a battle with the Crows and counted coup ahead of any grown man in the Lakota war party. This exploit won him the right to a man's name, and he became Sitting Bull.

Sitting Bull

From then on, he steadily advanced to the highest position of honor in the warrior society of the band. Warfare, always important among the Lakota, grew even more so as Sitting Bull became a mature leader. The pioneers had crowded eastern Indians onto the Plains, and the various tribes fought with new intensity and new weapons for the hunting grounds. Then, when white hunters began to slaughter buffalo by the tens of thousands just for their hides, Sitting Bull saw that his people must make a great decision.

He adopted a policy of peace and made a treaty with the United States government by which most of western South Dakota was set aside as a reservation for the Lakota. No white men except traders were to enter this area. The Lakota promised not to start any fighting—and they kept their promise until gold was discovered in the Black Hills. Immediately a gold rush began. Troops followed the miners. The Lakota lost no time in driving as many civilians and soldiers as they could off the reservation.

Newspapers in the East printed sensational stories about "outrages" committed by the Sioux, and feeling against them ran high. While the Army prepared to attack, General George Custer learned the whereabouts of five large bands of Sioux and moved against them with troops. But he had underestimated the ability of his foes. At the Little Big Horn River in 1876 the Sioux (with some Cheyennes) under the leadership of Sitting Bull and Crazy Horse wiped out Custer and all his men.

Sitting Bull realized that this victory, far from guaranteeing the security of the tribal lands, would provoke the United States Army to a full-scale war which the Sioux could never win. Acting not from cowardice, but from a desire to protect his people, Sitting Bull led them across the border to safety in Canada.

Years later he and his followers returned to the reservation in South Dakota. There, in the hope that the old Sioux virtues and spirit could be kept alive, Sitting Bull supported a religious revival that expressed itself in the Ghost Dance. The Government, fearing that the new religion would lead to new Indian outbreaks, ordered the arrest of Sitting Bull. Policemen who had been recruited from among the Sioux themselves came for the old man. Though he was unarmed, a scuffle followed, and the policemen shot and killed the stubborn leader who had never betrayed the interests of his people as he saw them.

Crazy Horse, a Sioux chief of South Dakota (?–1877). There are many stories about how Crazy Horse got his name. Some say it was because a wild pony ran loose through the village the night he was born. Others say it was because he was such an expert at gentling wild horses. Or just that his father was Crazy Horse, a wise medicine man of the Oglala Sioux.

Although he was several times defeated in battles with white troops who had better guns, Crazy Horse never gave up. He was daring and resourceful and combative to his last day. Once, after losing his band's horses to the United States Army, he took advantage of a blinding snowstorm, stampeded the animals, and got them all back.

Following the Battle of the Little Big Horn, the Army pursued him for a year and finally forced him, with two thousand of his people, onto a reservation. Though he was held under military guard, the fight had not even then gone out of him. He was shot and killed in an attempt to escape.

Cochise, a chief of the Chiricahua Apaches in Arizona and New Mexico (?–1874). Though the Chiricahua Apaches were habitual raiders of the nearby Mexicans, they had never bothered the more powerful Americans until the time of the Civil War. In 1861 a white child disappeared, and United States officers believed the Apaches were guilty of the kidnapping.

Seeing trouble ahead for his people, Cochise, with other chiefs, met the Americans under a flag of truce to assert the innocence of his band. The commanding officer ordered the chiefs arrested and bound. Cochise escaped by cutting his way out of the tent in which he was held, but his companions were all hanged.

Angered at what he considered treachery and injustice, Cochise then began a long war of revenge. Because so many Americans had left to take part in the Civil War, Cochise was able to spread terror in the Southwest for years. After the war, however, the soldiers returned and began systematic destruction of the Apaches. In 1871 Cochise surrendered. A year later, when his people were ordered to move from Arizona to New Mexico, he led eight hundred of his tribesmen in one last attempt at resistance. The Government responded by allowing the Apaches to stay on a reservation near their traditional home in Arizona. Cochise came there peacefully to join his people, and there he died.

Geronimo, a medicine man of the Chiricahua Apaches of Arizona (1829–1909). Apache resistance to white domination did not end with the death of Cochise. In fact, it flared up with new intensity within two years. In 1876 Geronimo, who had long been active against both Mexicans and Americans, led a group off the reservation. During much of the next ten years he fiercely harassed the growing number of settlers in the Southwest. At one time three thousand soldiers were assigned to hunt him down, and finally in 1886 he, together with seventy followers, was captured after a long pursuit. He and the entire Chiricahua band—men, women, and children— were then made military prisoners and held in Florida by the United States Army. The death rate among them was very high, and after great public protest the Chiricahuas were moved to Fort Sill, Oklahoma. There they remained prisoners of war—including the children born in prison—until 1914. Geronimo, leader of the last and most stubborn effort of Indians to keep their freedom, died at the age of eighty—still a prisoner.

Geronimo

Henry Roe-Cloud, a Winnebago of Nebraska (1884–1950). The ultimate release of the Apaches from their twenty-eight years of imprisonment was due largely to the efforts of another Indian, Henry Roe-Cloud, a Winnebago, born on a reservation in Nebraska. Roe-Cloud spoke only the language of his tribe until he was ten. Then he went away to school and became a skillful linguist, mastering not only English, but German, Spanish, Latin, Greek, and Hebrew. As a student at Yale he learned of the plight of the Apaches and organized the campaign that led to their freedom. In later life he spent many years as an official of the Bureau of Indian Affairs.

Chief Joseph, a Nez Percé chief of Oregon (?–1904). In 1836 the Nez Percé took the unusual step of inviting missionaries to come and educate them. They figured that since they were weaker than their traditional enemies, the Blackfeet, who in turn were weaker than the whites, they therefore would profit by the secret of the white man's strength. For forty years the Nez Percé had missionaries among them, and they lived at peace with the whites. But trouble developed when squatters moved onto their land and began to use force against the Indians. In 1877, Chief Joseph led his tribe in a war to keep possession of their beloved Wallowa Valley.

Chief Joseph

At first the Nez Percé won many battles. Then the United States Army came in such force that Chief Joseph saw there was no hope. To save his people from destruction, he led two hundred warriors and six hundred women and children on a thousand-mile retreat toward safety in Canada. The best-trained Army officers paid tribute to Joseph's brilliant generalship during his retreat. He made only one mistake in judgment. Thinking he had crossed into Canada, he ordered a rest for his weary followers. But the place where he stopped was just south of the border, and the troops surprised and captured him. Joseph was never allowed to return to his rich Wallowa Valley and died on a reservation in the State of Washington.

Washakie, a Shoshoni chief of Wyoming (c. 1804–1900). Reasoning in much the same way as the Nez Percé, the Shoshonis under their chief Washakie resolved to be friendly to the white man. They rounded up stray cattle for the pioneers who crossed their territory in covered wagons. They helped them to ford rivers and they acted as guides in strange country. Always they sought support from the settlers against the Crows, Blackfeet, and Sioux who pressed against them more and more heavily. At no time did the Shoshonis rise up against the Americans, although by 1878, when they had been forced onto a reservation, Washakie sometimes felt bitter and rebellious indeed. That year he spoke for all Indians and their distress at their cramped and difficult life on reservations, when he said to the Governor of Wyoming:

> The white man, who possesses this whole vast country from sea to sea, who roams over it at pleasure and lives where he likes, cannot know the cramp we feel in this little spot, with the undying remembrance of the fact, which you know as well as we, that every foot of what you proudly call America not very long ago belonged to the red man. . . . But the white man had, in ways we know not of, learned some things we had not learned; among them, how to make superior tools and terrible weapons, better for war than bows and arrows; and there seemed no end to the hordes of men that followed them from other lands beyond the sea.
>
> And so, at last, our fathers were steadily driven out, or killed, and we, their sons, but sorry remnants of tribes once mighty, are cornered in little spots of the earth all ours by right—cornered like guilty prisoners and watched by men with guns who are more than anxious to kill us off.
>
> Nor is this all. The white man's government promised that if we, the Shoshonis, would be content with the little patch allowed to us, it would keep us well supplied with everything necessary to comfortable living, and would see that no white man should cross our borders for our game or for anything that is ours. But it has not kept its word! The white man kills our game, captures our furs, and sometimes feeds his herds upon our meadows. And your great and mighty government—oh, sir, I hesitate, for I cannot tell the half! It

> does not protect us in our rights. It leaves us without the promised seed, without tools for cultivating the land, without implements for harvesting our crops . . . without the food we still lack, after all we can do . . . without the schools we so much need for our children. . . .
>
> Knowing all this, do you wonder, sir, that we have fits of desperation and think to be avenged?

What Washakie said for the Indians in 1878 was true—for that year and for many years after. Not until 1924 did Indians become American citizens, and it was 1948 before the last state removed its restrictions on their right to vote. Today, although Indians are increasingly a part of American life, they often are treated as second-class citizens. Even now new efforts are being made to take their remaining lands away from them.

Little by little, however, Indians are coming into their own. They no longer track deer through the woodlands or hunt buffalo on the great plains. They are shepherds, farmers, and factory workers, and since the Indian wars many of them have become prominent in American life.

Two men of mixed Indian-white ancestry have become Vice Presidents of the United States—John N. Garner, part Cherokee, and Charles Curtis, who had both Osage and Kaw ancestors.

The man who has the reputation of being the greatest all-round American athlete, Jim (James F.) Thorpe, was a Sauk Fox. In 1912 he made athletic history by winning every event in both the Decathlon and Pentathlon in the Olympic games. He has also been called the greatest of all football players and he played big-league baseball with the New York Giants.

Another big-league ball player of earlier years was "Chief" (Charles A.) Bender, a Chippewa, who pitched for the Philadelphia Athletics. When fans were rooting for the opposing team, they sometimes tried to rattle him by giving Indian war whoops. Chief Bender would walk close to the stands and shout scornfully "Foreigners!"

A more recent Indian headliner in baseball was Allie Reynolds, Yankee pitcher, who was a Creek. He died in 1994.

Will Rogers, the beloved humorist of the 1930s, was part Cherokee and grew up in Oklahoma where the Cherokees now live.

N. B. Johnson, a Cherokee, was the first president of the National Congress of American Indians, which represents all the various tribes in Washington, DC.

The Tallchief sisters, Maria and Marjorie, of the Osage Nation, are among the most talented and famous ballet dancers in America today. They founded the Chicago City Ballet in 1981.

Charles A. Eastman, Dakota, was a physician, the author of many books on Indian life, and a founder of the Boy Scouts. D'Arcy McNickle, Flathead, a novelist, wrote an excellent history of the Indian, *They Came Here First*. Maria Martinez, San Ildefonso, is world-famed for her beautiful pottery. And many other Indians have gained distinction as artists, writers, public servants, and authorities on Indian life.

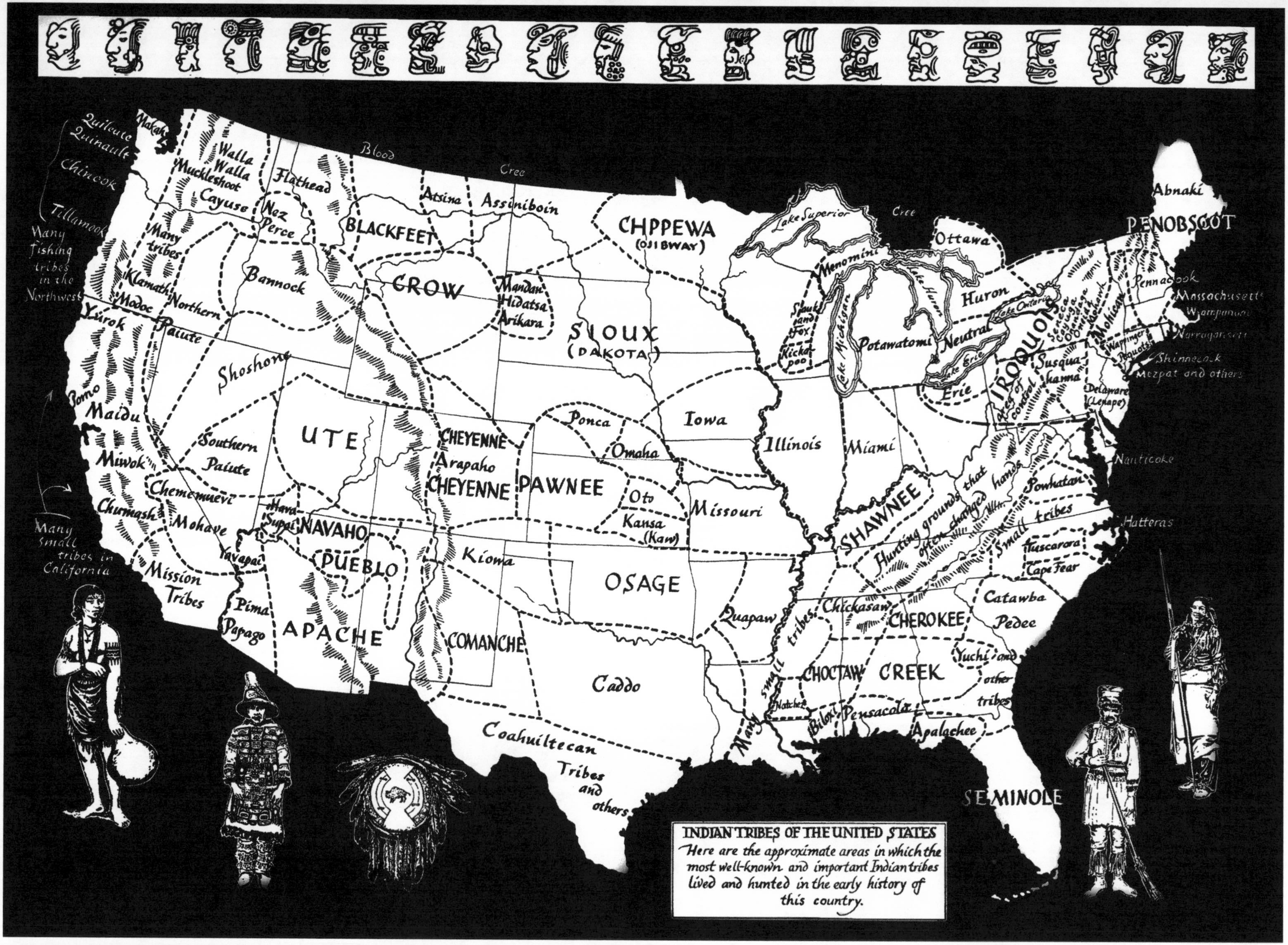

INDIAN TRIBES OF THE UNITED STATES

Here are the approximate areas in which the most well-known and important Indian tribes lived and hunted in the early history of this country.

Bibliography

The American Indian. An authoritative magazine emphasizing Indian affairs today.

Arizona Highways. A magazine that has published many articles about and excellent photographs of Arizona Indians, past and present.

Averill, Esther. *King Phillip,* Harper, 1950. A biography for young readers.

Baity, Elizabeth Chesley. *Americans Before Columbus,* Viking, 1951.

Boas, Franz. *The Central Eskimo,* Bureau of American Ethnology. Very scholarly, but also very readable.

Ceram, C. W. *Gods, Graves and Scholars,* Knopf, 1951. Contains an exciting chapter on Mayan archeological discoveries.

Cohen, Felix. *Handbook of Federal Indian Law,* US Government Printing Office, 1942.

Collier, John. *Indians of the Americas,* Norton, 1947; abridged, New American Library, 1952.

Cotterill, R. S. *The Southern Indians; the Story of the Civilized Tribes before Removal,* University of Oklahoma Press, 1954.

Debo, Angie. *And Still the Waters Run,* Princeton University Press, 1940.

Denver Art Museum, Department of Indian Art, publishes over 100 illustrated leaflets on special aspects of Indian material culture.

Douglas, Frederic H., And D'harnoncourt, René. *Indian Art of the United States,* Simon & Schuster, 1948.

Eastman, Charles. *Indian Boyhood,* E. M. Hale, Wisconsin (Cadmus Books). Authentic autobiographical account of boyhood among the Sioux.

Embree, Edwin Rogers. *Indians of the Americas,* Houghton, 1939.

Ethnic Folkways has long-playing records of Sioux and Navaho music.

Fast, Howard. *The Last Frontier,* Due11, Sloan & Pearce, 1941.

Foreman, Grant. *Advancing the Frontier,* University of Oklahoma Press, 1933. The story of Indians after they arrived in Oklahoma.

———. *The Five Civilized Tribes,* University of Oklahoma Press, 1934.

———. *Indian Removal,* University of Oklahoma Press, 1932, 1953.

———. *Sequoyah,* University of Oklahoma Press, 1938.

———. *The Last Trek of the Indians,* University of Chicago Press, 1946.

Gessner, Robert. *Massacre,* Farrar, 1931.

Gilpin, Laura. *The Pueblos; A Camera Chronicle,* Hastings House, 1942.

Gorham, Michael. *The Real Book About Indians,* Garden City, 1953. For young readers, but accurate and interesting for all age levels.

Graham, Shirley. *The Story of Pocahontas,* Grosset & Dunlap, 1953.

Grinnell, George Bird. *Cheyenne Indians: Their History and Ways of Life,* Yale University Press, 1923.

Grinnell, George Bird. *Pawnee Hero Stories and Folk Tales,* Scribner.

Hamilton, Charles, editor. *Cry of the Thunderbird; the American Indian's Own Story,* Macmillan, 1950. A fascinating collection of writings by Indians.

Hannum, Alberta. *Spin a Silver Dollar,* Viking, 1945. The story of a young Navaho artist.

Hibben, Frank C. *Treasure in the Dust; Exploring Ancient North America,* Lippincott, 1951.

Hodge, Frederick W., editor. *Handbook of American Indians North of Mexico,* Bureau of American Ethnology, 1907, 1910. A two-volume detailed source book.

James, George Wharton. *Indian Blankets and Their Makers,* University of Chicago Press, 1927.

Kent, Rockwell. *Salamina,* Harcourt, 1935. Beautiful illustrations and text about modern Eskimos of Greenland.

La. Farge, Oliver. *As Long as the Grass Shall Grow,* Longmans, 1941.

———. (editor) *The Changing Indian,* University of Oklahoma Press, 1942.

———. *Cochise of Arizona,* Aladdin Books, 1953. A biography for young readers.

———. *Enemy Gods,* Houghton, 1937.

Laubin, Gladys and Reginald. Appear throughout the country in recitals of authentic Indian dances.

The Library of Congress has produced several long-playing records of Indian music.

Lockwood, Frank C. *The Apache Indians,* Macmillan, 1938.

Lucas, Jannette May. *Indian Harvest: Wild food plants of the first Americans,* Lippincott, 1945.

Mccombe, Leonard; Vogt, Evon Z.; and Kluckhohn, Clyde. *Navaho Means People,* Harvard University Press, 1951. A serious text with beautiful photographs.

Mcnickle, D'arcy. *They Came Here First,* Lippincott, 1949. A history of the Indians.

Marriott, Alice. *Greener Fields,* Crowell, 1953. Lively personal reminiscences of an anthropologist who has lived among present-day Indians.

———. *María, the Potter of San Ildefonso,* University of Oklahoma Press, 1948.

Marriott, Alice. *Ten Grandmothers,* University of Oklahoma Press, 1945.

Meadowcroft, Enid Lamonte. *The Story of Crazy Horse,* Grosset & Dunlap, 1954.

Morris, Ann Axtell. *Digging in Yucatan,* Doubleday, 1931. A very human narrative of archeological excavation in the land of the Mayas.

National Park Service pamphlets of special interest: *Aztec Ruins National Monument; Chaco Canyon National Monument; Wupatki National Monument; Navaho National Monument; Mound City Group National Monument.*

O'Kane, Walter Collins. *The Hopis: Portrait of a Desert People,* University of Oklahoma Press, 1953.

Parker, Arthur C. *The Indian How Book,* Doran, 1927. Information about Indian woodcraft; how Indians made and did a great many things.

———. *Red Jacket: Last of the Seneca,* McGraw-Hill, 1952. A biography for young readers.

Radin, Paul. *The Story of the American Indian,* Liveright, 1944. An anthropologist surveys Indian culture.

Sandoz, Mari. *Cheyenne Autumn,* McGraw-Hill, 1953.

Starkey, Marion L. *Cherokee Nation,* Knopf, 1946. A very readable history based on sound scholarship.

Stefansson, Vilhjalmur. *Hunters of the Great North,* Harcourt, 1922. On Eskimos.

———. *My Life with the Eskimo,* Macmillan, 1951.

Swanton, John R. *The Indian Tribes of North America,* Bureau of American Ethnology, 1952. A detailed reference book, useful for looking up Indian tribes, villages, or place names in specific localities.

Tompkins, William. *Universal Indian Sign Language.* Clear explanations with illustrations.

Underhill, Ruth. *Here Come the Navaho.*

———. "Indian, American," an article in the World Book Encyclopedia. Excellent for young readers.

———. *Indians of the Pacific Northwest,* US Indian Service, 1945.

———. The Northern Paiute.

Underhill, Ruth. *People of the Crimson Sunset.* On the Papagos.

———. *Red Man's America,* University of Chicago Press, 1953. The most recent and best history of the Indians.

———. *Workaday Life of the Pueblos,* US Indian Service.

Vaillant, George Clapp. *Aztecs of Mexico,* Doubleday 1941.

Vestal, Stanley. *Sitting Bull,* Houghton, 1932. The best biography.

Wellman, Paul I. *The Indian Wars of the West,* Doubleday, 1954. A detailed history.

White, Anne Terry. *Prehistoric America,* Random House, 1951. For young readers.

Wissler, Clark. *Indians of the United. States,* Doubleday, 1940. A standard general book.

Wormington, H. M. *Prehistoric Indians of the Southwest,* Denver Museum of Natural History, 1947. A good summary by a specialist.

Index

C

F

G

H